My POV

Jim Charles

Published by Donahue Publishing

First Edition

ISBN: 979-8-89864-025-5

For information about special discounts for bulk purchases, please contact Donahue Publishing at info@donahuepublishing.co.

www.donahuepublishing.co

Contents

Chapter 1

In the absence of light, the only audible sounds were voices, intermittently fading.

A male voice, distant and urgent: "Did you reach her grandmother?"

A female voice, hesitant: "About that, sir..."

Another female voice, whispering: "Did you hear the rumor?"

The first woman again, shocked: "She what?! No way... what happened?"

Where was I? How long have I been here? Why do I feel empty?

A different male voice: "How long has it been?"

Another man responds: "Jesus, I don't know."

A woman's voice, barely audible: "Believe me, she is..."

Someone else murmurs: "Poor thing."

I couldn't stay in here. Please, somebody help! The voices were driving me crazy. They kept coming and fading. It went on like that for quite a while. Then, when all hope was lost, I felt a light reaching me. At that moment, I was able to open my eyes. I was welcomed by a bright light that blinded me. I blinked my eyes to clear my sight. To my biggest surprise, I was lying on a hospital bed. My body felt numb; I was welcomed by the pungent smell of hospital disinfectant invading my nostrils. I glanced around the deserted blue and white room of the hospital. Then my eyes fell on someone wonderful.

"Glad to see you're okay," Amadaniel said softly.

I tried to speak, but my mouth was dry. He went ahead: "Take it easy."

I couldn't believe it; I couldn't be any happier to see him. With his presence alone, he managed to bring my mind at ease. He always found a way to be there when it mattered the most. He had a gift for knowing how to lift me up. With my body still aching, he rearranged the pillow and helped me put my torso in an upright position so I could sit. I was content to have him close to me. Amadaniel sat down and didn't say a word—he just held my hand. I will always remember those moments when I was lost in the depths of the sea—he was my anchor in that treacherous water. He was the best person I knew on this planet, from the depths of his eyes to the gentle expressions of his voice. He was unique in his truthful opinions. I loved the way his voice quickened when he sparkled with a new idea or was enjoying one of mine, but something felt different. Goosebumps crossed my entire body when I felt his hand being so cold and trembling.

"Glad to see you," I whispered.

He squeezed my hand. I could see he was holding back his tears. Then, with a broken voice, he asked me, "What happened?"

I was confused by his question. I got even more confused when I tried to remember what situation brought me here, but it was blank—no matter how hard I tried.

"I... I... I don't know."

I could see in his eyes that something bad had occurred, but I couldn't recall anything. I could feel his heart cracking like glass—a lone tear traced down his cheek.

"Are you okay?"

Then the floodgates opened. I could hardly bear the sight of his sadness, but the tears were letting me know the fear, the pain, the stress that was consuming him. It felt as if the world had gone dark, like a big curtain being pulled across the sky. Tears streaming down his cheeks, falling like raindrops. I didn't know what to say or do—I simply told him with a heartbreaking voice:

"I'm sorry."

My POV

I couldn't believe what I was witnessing—it was the first time I saw him this vulnerable. The doctor entered the room, and Amadaniel let go of my hand, looked away, and wiped his tears.

"I need a moment with her," the doctor said.

He got up, leaned towards me, and gave me a kiss on the forehead before leaving the room. Alone with the doctor, he started talking to me, but his voice was distorted. I was getting dizzy—everything started to move in the room. The more he talked, the more the room spun. I was about to throw up. When he closed my file, everything went back to normal. He sat next to me.

"You're persistent for a failure," he said with cold calculation.

"What?"

"Why don't you do us both a favor and die?"

"Excuse me?"

I didn't like the tone he was using. He was talking to me with pure contempt. He was crude, dry, and mean. He took my wrist in his hands and examined it carefully—then suddenly his grip tightened as the lights began to flicker. I instantly screamed at him, "Let go of me!"

But there was no response—he lifted his head, and when he laid his eyes on me, black fluid was dripping from every orifice of his face. I was paralyzed by terror. I could feel the pressure he was applying to my wrists, but the horror I was facing disabled me from feeling the pain. In a distorted voice, he screamed, "DIE!"

That scream was accompanied by a screeching, awful noise. Unable to move a muscle, he went ahead to violently rip my bandages that were covering my wrists. Underneath them, there were deep lacerations. I didn't even have a second to comprehend what was going on. The doctor applied pressure to my wounds by sticking his sharp, razor-like nails in them and squeezing them like sponges. In excruciating pain, I screamed, "Stop!"

He suddenly stopped, but I couldn't move an inch. Petrified on the bed, I could only keep my eyes on whatever was happening in front of me. He had no eyes, no nose, no eyebrows—nothing besides an evil smile that went all the way up his cheeks. He had a mouth filled with sharp teeth. He tilted his head to the side, lifted his finger, and put it on my lips. In this surreal situation, he sewed my lips shut. Then he went on, digging furiously into my lacerations until my hand fell off. My blood squirted in profusion all over the place—everything turned red. The room was filled with my blood. He grabbed my face while sticking every nail into it before slowly gouging out my eyes. The last thing I saw with my trembling iris was his face melting before hearing his wretched laugh.

"WAKE UP! WAKE UP!" Amadaniel's voice cut through the nightmare.

I opened my eyes, screaming my heart out. By my side was Amadaniel.

"I can't breathe! Help me!"

"Easy... easy, don't worry. I'm here. Listen to me—breathe."

I followed his instructions and took a few deep breaths. Everything went back to normal. I trembled in fear—Amadaniel took me in his arms and hugged me so hard that it calmed me down, but this nightmare was so vivid I couldn't erase it from my mind. I managed to regain my senses. He put his hands on my shoulders, reassuring me with his usual comforting smile. As I finally relaxed and let my guard down, the lights started to flicker, attracting my attention. Then I started to feel pressure on my shoulders—it was so strong I could feel my bones crack. The room got colder in an instant. My eyes lay—in panic—on my friend's face. He said in a vile tone, "Death suits you better."

A sordid smirk was plastered across his face. I could see his sharp, yellow teeth. He laughed while inserting his long nails into my shoulders. In agony, my friend's face slowly burned alive in front of me while he continued holding me. The heat was unbearable—he was making my skin peel off. I couldn't look away—I watched his flesh fall off as he made an awful scream, making my ears and eyes bleed.

The sprinklers activated—the water was cold. I could hear the walls cracking. They were on the verge of collapsing. The sound of the water got louder and louder—water started erupting from everywhere, then, under the intense pressure, everything collapsed, letting out a thunderous sound. The pressure of the water crushed me, filling my lungs in an instant—not able to breathe, I once more reached a place of total darkness.

Chapter 2

Time. The continuous progression of existence that occurs in an apparently irreversible succession from the past, through the present, and into the future. Time knows no limit. We have zero control over it, yet time is slow when you wait, time is fast when you are late, while time is short when you are happy, and time can even stand still when you are in pain. Inside this eternal flow, we are just a dot.

"Hey, love, go ahead and eat," Mom said.

"Yes, sorry, I was on the moon," I replied as a little girl.

My dad prepared the table. It was marvelous—a nice, tender piece of chicken was waiting for me with some vegetables on the side.

"Thanks, Dad," I said.

"My pleasure," he replied with a warm smile.

While we were eating, my dad was entertaining us by making me laugh in his usual way. Then the phone rang, and Dad picked it up. As he was chatting on the phone, he kept looking at me with a huge smile. He pulled his tongue out while listening to his interlocutor. When the conversation ended, Dad came to finish his dinner with us. My dad was lost in thought, worried that he had received bad news. He looked at me with a warm smile and said, "Wow, I was on the moon."

When we were done, someone knocked at the door. My dad looked at my mom before getting up to open the door. She didn't say a word to him. She got up and told me that tonight I would be eating my dessert in my room. Before leaving us, my dad kissed me on the forehead and left the room. On my way to my room, I tried to have a glimpse of who was at the door, but my mom caught me and told me to go to my room or else no dessert. I ran to my room and waited for her to bring me my sweet. After a moment, my mom came to my room, sat next to me on my bed, and gave me my dessert.

"Who's at the door?" I asked.

"A friend of Dad's," Mom answered softly.

"Why can't I see him?" I pressed.

"Because it's late," she said, tucking my hair behind my ear.

She kissed me on the forehead and wished me goodnight before leaving the room. Before falling asleep, I ate my dessert. In the morning, my nose was charmed by an herbaceous smell. It was my grandmother's morning tea. I got up and went downstairs. I salivated with each step I was taking. The smell of fresh, warm, buttery bread was seducing my nostrils. My grandmother was at the table listening to the news. Once again, war was the topic.

As I grew older, I asked myself: how would the world be if it were perfect? Would it be peaceful, where everyone lived comfortably and happily? Or would we be empty shells—creatures living without the impulse of sins? Sins that we love and yet hate so much. So many questions without answers—only speculation, hypotheses created by the train of my imagination. We experience life differently under the same tree; so many paths in our journey. From the soil to the very top, we keep growing, but to what end?

I know we are creatures guided by emotion. We are affected by who we meet, by what we say, hear, and do—everything that makes us good or bad, what makes us cry or laugh, what makes us love or hate. All those moments create our story, our timeline. We are built for the better and the worst. We have flaws, we have many reasons to be who we are, but we also have the possibility to bypass those basic instincts and live for a better purpose.

I know I make it sound simple—call me optimistic or delusional—but we do not need to drown each other just to have the opportunity to set our eyes toward the same sky. If we could use our strength for the greater good, those drowning in deep, dark seas wouldn't have to swim in despair to chase the surface like a distant dream. Together, we could easily make the impossible possible, in the same motion, saving ourselves from our own demise. Even after saying all this, what is the beauty of life?

As time flies, I learn that we all could be better. We have the power to bring light to those close and far from us. Instead, we let malice roam without punishment. We decide to drown each other with fear by pretending we do not have other choices and call that freak show "human nature." We can all breathe the same air.

What's dead can be reborn, what's lost can be found, what's destroyed can be rebuilt. We can stare together toward the infinite possibilities that life gave us under one tree. We are letting many souls drown, killing in the process the roots of what we could become. What shatters me is the fact that we manage to stay blind to this concept. Why? Lack of devotion? Ambition? Wonderment?

"Psst... Time to go to school, young lady," Grandmother called softly.

Oh snap! I looked at the clock—I couldn't believe how fast time passed when you least expected it. I took a few quick bites of the delicious breakfast prepared by my wonderful grandmother, shoving everything down with a full glass of orange juice.

"I'll take care of the rest, just don't be late again," Grandmother said with a knowing smile.

A quick kiss of thanks. I ran to the entrance, grabbed my navy blue coat from the wooden coat rack. Crossing the door, I was welcomed by a nice breeze caressing my skin with a gentle touch—it was refreshing, and the weather was beautiful. Autumn came with regal ease, content to arrive with slow grace. I was jogging towards my destination, in the middle of a red and gold parade. The weather had been marvelous, like summer was not done. Unfortunately, a storm was supposed to be heading towards us—from what people are saying, it might be a violent one.

To save time to reach the bus, I took a shortcut by taking the abandoned road near my home, crossing a white wooden bridge facing a nearby small waterfall that was coming all the way from the mountain and flowing down to the river. Not many people use that road anymore since they built a tunnel through the mountain. The road had lain over the earth for as long as anyone could remember. It had been so many years since they closed this passage, making nature reclaim it in her own suitable time. The roots grew in, over the grey concrete that was almost not visible with all the grass, making the land gain a second breath.

Reaching my stop in advance, I had time to catch my breath. I sat on the bench with my bag next to me, and I looked at the sky after taking a good inhalation of fresh air. I could see the sunshine and gray clouds battling against each other from afar. The locals said the sky would turn mad, letting rain beat down our flamboyant trees, accompanied by lightning and thunder to play for us mere mortals a unique composition. We would receive enough rain to flood a lot of areas; sheets of water would be falling from the sky like someone forgot to close the faucet up there. Wind strong enough to shake down the biggest trees. Everyone was cautioned about the upcoming disaster—you know the saying: better safe than sorry—so to be prepared, many walls of sandbags were put in various locations to prevent any major damage, and stores and houses were barricaded. People were on edge—the last time they announced weather like this, it was a tragic day for a lot of people, especially me. Even though it brought me pain, I couldn't look away from the patches of light shyly hiding beneath the sheet of gray clouds that had the same color as steel. The white leading edge was beautiful—it seemed with the tip of my finger I could turn a new page. It was an impressive sight.

Then the horn of the bus snapped me from my gaze. Once on the bus, I was greeted by Jacob, the bus driver—he was always listening to the news on the radio. Walking to my usual spot, I saw that a few students were absent this morning. With the announcement of the upcoming storm, many wanted to avoid being trapped in this unpleasant scenario. The news report said it should be above us in a few days. I sat down, putting my bag on my lap. Looking at the empty seat next to me, I couldn't stop myself from thinking about my best friend—since the accident, I wasn't able to get in touch with him, and it worried me. He always sat next to me, leaving the window side for me, knowing how easily I get lost in my thoughts—he was so thoughtful of my needs that it would be a relaxing way to travel with the view of a nice landscape. Mystified by the wonderful countryside, my mind and body were disconnected from the world—I had trouble stopping my train of thought, and it didn't take me long to be lost in it.

In a gloomy mood, I couldn't stop thinking about the day we met—it was a warm memory from one of the saddest times of my childhood. Everything went downhill after the death of my parents—it seems cliché, but nonetheless, I was devastated, hurt, and betrayed by the harsh reality I was exposed to in the adult world. What I lived through scarred me at such a youthful age—money has a way of creating emotional indifference between people, replacing love and gratitude. In doing so, it decreases the proper development of empathy and creativity in the prefrontal cortex. This type of brain damage I was subjected to caught me off guard. A few weeks after the loss of my parents, there was a meeting in my mom's office.

During those last few weeks, even though a tragedy of that size had befallen me, everything was magical. Even though I was torn apart, those around me brought comfort and eased my pain. I couldn't ask for better—the way they were talking about my parents blew me away. All those anecdotes brought a smile in those troubled times. I was fascinated to see how many people knew and loved them. I didn't realize I was only placing a bandage on a wound that needed more, but it made me mourn without the feeling of being abandoned.

Sadly, during that meeting, a man with a suitcase asked everyone to gather in the office. One of my uncles was furious—I heard his scream in the hall. Then boom! I heard a door being slammed. I approached the scene. The door was left ajar, and I heard people arguing. I leaned an attentive ear to the conversation to finally understand why Grandma told me, "Not every adult business is for children."

I was part of an ignoble charade, and I was the main character in that tragedy. One by one, they all left the room after hearing what needed to be said—they all had dissatisfied expressions glued to their faces—and what had been familiar and friendly faces became rude and annoyed. I stood there as they walked by, all smiling and pretending I didn't witness grown-ups using hateful words about my late parents over something so trivial as money and materials. I had no one to speak with—those impostors took pity on me only for their personal gain, looking after me like a wounded puppy that they could heal with sweet words. After being exposed to this unhealthy sight, I retreated into my parents' library. I didn't know how to feel—I was lost and confused, trying to figure out what just happened.

I sat there in a room where the words kept silent. The pitiful bandage was ripped, letting grief engulf me. Trying to deny this emotion, I took a book to let my mind wander elsewhere. The air in the room was cold and empty, when then a distant echo resonated in my head.

"Love?" Grandma's voice called from somewhere distant.

"... Love?" she called again, closer now.

I couldn't move a muscle; I couldn't even utter a word. I had been trampled upon by pretenders—I kept reading the same sentence over and over, trying to make sense of the unknown. I completely shut down; I knew this because that was the last memory I had before waking up in my bed. The days that came after were an unbearable show. My grandmother tried her best to shield me from those greedy feuds that were forming around the death of my parents. She was overwhelmed by the situation, but for my sake, she did what must be done. One by one, they stopped being polite and showed their true faces behind those magnificent jester masks—but regardless of how many times they tried to approach me, Grandma stood her ground. To this day, I know it was about money, but with how things quickly went south, it must be for something else. It had to be.

I regret that I was able to understand the perversion of life at such an early age. It affected me, making me grow up distancing myself from people, mostly adults at first, but as I kept retreating, it was projected onto everyone. I built a shield thick enough to protect me from any harm. After months had passed, I managed to have a sense of clarity when I met my friend Amadaniel. I remember it like it was yesterday. It was a sublime afternoon, where the sun was singing and the flowers in return praised him for his warmth by dancing in harmony with the passage of a serene breeze. This day, during our recess, I was disturbed during my usual reading by a shadow that was hovering over me. I didn't want to interact with whoever was there—I closed my book to change locations, but like an eclipse, the light slowly came back. Then I heard a soothing laugh before hearing for the first time a generous voice apologizing to me.

"Excuse me, I didn't want to block your light," the boy said.

As I lifted my head, he bent over to pick up something next to me. My eyes following his hand, I saw him pick up a ball that was next to me. I was so focused on my reading that I didn't notice that a ball had fallen next to me. I raised my head to see who owned that voice, but before I could lay eyes on him, a bunch of students came rushing towards my location, celebrating. Without the care to acknowledge my presence, I was caught inside this gathering. I tried to get out by crawling out of there, but I got stepped on on my hand. Enough pressure was put on it to make me drop a few tears. On my knees, I tried to get up, but the crowd was too agitated to allow me to properly stand. My misadventure stopped abruptly when I heard once more that generous voice.

"I have the ball. Let's go back!" the same boy called out firmly.

Like a real leader, he commanded his troupe with ease. As I watched them leave, Jerry turned around and gave me a grimace, letting me know he knew I was there. They all went back to the playground; tranquillity came back without further misfortune.

My POV

Wiping my tears, I wiped the dirt off me. Without paying more mind to what had just occurred, I went back to my book, letting my curiosity for this unknown boy fade away so I could bathe in my imagination. Those moments of quiet were delightful to my ears. We had an amazing librarian; she was kind enough to let me read books from her personal library. The ones we had in school were neither educational nor interesting enough. She saw my interest in more sophisticated lectures, so she introduced me to all kinds of books from her personal collection.

Chapter 3

The memory pulls me deeper as the bus rocks gently forward. I close my eyes and let myself fall back into that day when everything changed.

On my way to school, I was keeping my eyes on the landscape in a world where conflicts happen more often than they should. I kept reminiscing about that recess that made me walk away from a dark path. Even now, years later, I can still feel the weight of that moment, the way it shifted something fundamental inside me.

My book done, I walked back to school to borrow another one from the librarian, Miss Jane. Walking towards school, I was halted by a group of students who gathered near the entrance. I quickly slid through the students like a swift snake. This was my usual strategy. Invisible. Untouchable. Safe.

Progressing towards the door, I could hear one of my classmates arguing with someone, but having no desire to see this infantile quarrel, I pressed my movement. The crowd became tense, and I was struggling to keep moving at my will. I got pushed away from my destination, and the wave of students kept coming until I was moved to the front row of the herd.

I should have fought harder to escape. But something kept me there, frozen between curiosity and dread.

I looked to my left and my right to see that a circle was made. I turned around, and there were two people in the middle of this circle. The one that I was facing was Phil Corvet, but the other person who was standing in front of him didn't ring a bell. Yet something about his posture, his calm, felt familiar. Before I could scrutinize him, Phil gave me a little jump scare when he shouted, "We lost because you are a cheater!"

The boy in front of him responded. It was the same voice of the shadow underneath the tree. The voice that had apologized for blocking my light. It was also the same voice that suggested that the celebration had been moved somewhere else. Then, in a sarcastic way, he replied with no worry to Phil, "I am sorry, next time I'll let you win."

Even in the middle of confrontation, his voice carried that same gentle quality. I found myself leaning forward, despite every instinct telling me to disappear.

Students started to laugh. I could see in Phil's face that he didn't like how the response was welcomed by cheers of amusement. Phil clenched his fists and rubbed his thumbs against his fingers, trying to keep his composure. When he was starting to get in that state, it was hard to keep him under control.

I knew that look. I'd seen it before. The moment when someone decides that words aren't enough anymore.

Those who were having a good laugh quickly received a death stare from Phil. The laughter died like someone had turned off a switch. I could hear some of them swallowing their saliva out of fear. With minimum effort, he succeeded in intimidating an entire group of students.

Then something unexpected arrived. As Phil opened his mouth to give a rebuttal, a small fly flew inside his mouth. Having the best place in the crowd, I saw him swallow the poor little insect like it was nothing. For one impossible moment, I felt my lips twitch. Was that... was I about to smile?

He coughed, then scanned his surroundings to see if anyone had noticed that bestial act. Laying his eyes on me, I could see anger rising. The moment our eyes met, I realized my mistake. I had let my guard down. I had allowed myself to feel something other than fear.

He started walking towards me, with his eyebrows furrowing. Each step felt like a countdown to my destruction. In the passage, he bumped his shoulder against his opponent while keeping his eyes on me with a burning glare of anger. He used an intimidating tone to remind everyone that he was not the type of person you wanted to mess with and said:

"Why are you laughing, stupid weirdo?" Phil demanded.

The words hit me like a physical blow. Laughing. Had I been laughing? I didn't remember laughing. I hadn't laughed in... how long? Months? Years?

That unsolicited confrontation made me tremble to my core. I was shocked when Phil told me I was laughing. It was an expression I hadn't felt for a long time. How could something slip past my defenses like that? How could I have let myself be so vulnerable?

Phil standing in front of me paralyzed me. I just wanted to make myself invisible. I was vulnerable, and I didn't know how to act. I spent much time avoiding confrontation, rejecting the adult drama and whoever looked to harm my peace, but by doing so, I went into downfall.

This was what happened when you let your guard down. This was why I built my walls so high.

I gave a cold shoulder to anyone who approached me. I wouldn't be tainted by the hypocrisy of this world. For the way I conducted myself, I was mocked, and with that, I was bullied, but I didn't care. I made my peace with this wretched globe. My books became my sole ally. I built a sturdy shield, and before I knew it, I became my own shadow.

I didn't feel I belonged with any of them. Was I wrong to act like that? Was I really making my life less miserable? Was I nourishing my fear with past trauma? These questions swirled through my mind even as Phil closed the distance between us.

I wanted him to leave me alone. I wanted everyone to disappear. Looking down, my legs were shaking. I was ready to drop to my knees as the air started to feel heavy. How could I laugh without realizing it? Was I that far gone in my despair?

Phil was imposing for his age. That's why none dared to challenge him, until that day. People didn't care that my knees were clapping against each other. They were only amused and passing hurtful comments since the threat wasn't on them.

I was drowning in front of everyone, and they were treating it like entertainment.

Then suddenly I heard a voice say, "Hey, leave her alone!"

The voice cut through my panic like a lifeline thrown into churning water. Someone was standing up for me. Someone I barely knew was willing to face Phil Corvet for my sake.

Phil looked over his shoulder. Without laying an eye on me, he swung the palm of his hand towards my face. With no time to react, I closed my eyes and braced for the impact, but he never connected.

The world seemed to stop.

I opened my eyes and I saw that Phil's wrist was caught by his foe. From there, a battle of strength appeared. They were both pulling their arms towards their bodies, but none of them was giving an edge to the other.

In that moment, watching this stranger protect me, something cracked inside the shell I'd built around myself.

After a moment, Phil managed to break free from his hold. Then, with a strong, two-handed push, he brought his adversary to the ground. He gently rubbed his wrist and grimaced a little. It seemed his dance partner had an iron grip.

Phil, proud of his feat, unleashed a victorious scream while lifting his arms in the air, sending the crowd ablaze. In a position of dominance, Phil cast his shadow on his opponent. Phil looked at me and his adversary back and forth, then pointed his finger at me while looking at his challenger and burst into laughter, then he said arrogantly and with disgust:

"You love this weirdo, newbie?" Phil taunted.

The words should have stung. They should have sent me deeper into my shell. But watching this boy get up, brush off the dust, and look Phil in the eye with that same calm expression... something was changing inside me.

He slowly got up and removed the dust from himself, unfazed by the raw strength of Phil. The crowd teased me as they were blowing kisses and shouting, exposed by this ridiculous claim. Everyone was entertained by this squabble, waiting impatiently for the next scene.

Why did he stand up for me? We never spoke to each other. What did he want? Did he know me? Did he have a hero complex?

But maybe, just maybe, those weren't the right questions. Maybe the question was: when was the last time someone had shown me kindness without expecting anything in return?

People tended to not approach me. I made sure of that. I took the label of weirdo with pride and never looked back. Everyone avoided me like I was the plague. I won't be tricked by anyone.

His skinny stature made me wonder even more about his motives. Fighting someone heavier than you was mostly a disadvantage, but like anything, there were always pros and cons. Lighter guys tended to be quicker and faster on their feet, which should often nullify a power advantage, but he didn't look like that type. It was already a miracle that he was able to hold Phil's wrist that long.

Still, he didn't seem to be afraid of his opponent. Did he have something up his sleeve? Fearless, he looked at Phil straight in the eyes and gave him a smirk with an untroubled look on his face.

And in that fearlessness, I saw something I'd forgotten existed. Hope.

The crowd was getting more agitated by this display of boldness. Everyone knew that Phil wouldn't walk away quietly. Not after his authority was directly challenged in front of everyone. His ego wouldn't allow that. That level of confrontation only meant that the new guys wanted to be the new bosses of this place. That alone was good enough for Phil to make the bells of the chapel ring for those who opposed him.

I should have looked away. I should have slipped back into the crowd and disappeared. But I couldn't. For the first time in months, I was witnessing someone stand up to the darkness that ruled our world.

Pleased by the spectacle, the flock was craving for a severe beat-down. The populace waited impatiently for some development.

He lifted his arms and got into a fighting stance against Phil. He started to skip left and right without removing his eyes from Phil. With no stress in his body language, he clenched his fists with a smile glued to his face. Was he taunting him, or was he crazy? Maybe he was trying to force him to make a false move or play mind tricks?

Whatever his strategy, it was working. And something about his confidence, his refusal to be intimidated, made my heart beat differently.

Either way, it seemed it was working, because Phil was boiling with rage. Phil charged, and his nemesis evaded this frontal attack and replied with a couple of punches that his opponents had no issue handling with their large bodies.

The students had trouble holding in much thrill. They were about to see something unprecedented. The clash would be talked about for days, weeks, even months, regardless of the outcome.

But for me, this wasn't entertainment. This was someone choosing to fight for what was right, even when it cost him. This was what courage looked like.

In proximity, Phil grabbed his foe but didn't expect a quick counterattack. He received an elbow to the eye, which made him release his hold. A window just opened for the newbie. He went for the final blow, but Phil wasn't out of this fight as he blocked the strike and replied with a hard punch to the stomach.

After this exchange, they both took a few steps back. The frenzy in the air was breathtaking. Both having no intention of giving up, they stared at each other.

In that moment of stillness, our eyes met across the circle. And I saw something that changed everything. Recognition. Not of who I was, but of what I was feeling. He understood.

Then suddenly, a student shouted:

"Principal O'Neal! O'Neal is coming!"

The crowd completely dispersed in a matter of seconds, leaving only dust behind them. The only one left was my savior. He was standing right in front of me, rubbing his neck with a tender smile that was genuinely soothing.

We were alone now. Just the two of us in the space where violence had been moments before. And instead of the usual panic I felt when trapped with another person, I felt... curious.

As I kept my eyes on him, I tried to see what type of mask he was wearing. I didn't want or need to be deceived by other smiles full of lies and malice. I was already tarnished. Did I need to see everyone as an enemy? Why should I trust him? Why should I talk to him? Would he hurt me?

But even as these questions raced through my mind, I knew something was different. The way he'd fought wasn't about winning. It was about protecting. The way he looked at me now wasn't with pity or disgust. It was with... understanding.

A heavy silence was building between us. Unable to find answers to those questions, I let my eyes wander around until my attention was brought towards a colony of ants transporting food. I couldn't even thank him for his intervention. I stood there nervously, caressing my hands.

I couldn't make a simple interaction with another human being. I had been in my own bubble for so long that I had forgotten how to interact. I was incapable of dropping a single word. My wounds made me rotten from the inside.

My POV

Facing that crisis, I remained silent. Why should he be different than the others? I would rather become, to his eyes, what everyone thought of me. An outcast, a dead product of society, a loner. No matter what his intentions were, they seemed futile. I don't have any expectations. This world can't be good without a heavy price, so I won't break now and be fooled by this masquerade.

But then something happened that shattered all my carefully constructed defenses.

With a calm and joyful voice, I could hear sadness trembling behind his words:

"It's okay to laugh," he said gently.

Four simple words. But they reached into the deepest part of my soul and touched something I thought was dead forever.

His words went through the very core of my soul. I was touched by this show of humility. It felt like he saw the anvil of pain that I was carrying. He showed me he had the heart to bring comfort and extend himself to the needs of others. I was struggling to give him a token of my appreciation because I was on the verge of breaking up in tears.

He didn't say I was weird for laughing. He didn't mock me or ignore what had happened. He gave me permission to be human again.

I had been traveling in this dark tunnel where seeing light wasn't even a dream. He acknowledged my pain without taking pity on me. Before I could put my mind to commit to one of the five basics of communication, shouting was coming our way.

Timothy arrived behind the man of the hour and locked his head under his arm and told him, before releasing him, that recess wasn't over and that his skills were most needed, begging him to join him back on the field. Then Timothy sprinted away from us.

I watched this interruption with something close to panic. He was about to leave. This moment, this connection, would be over, and I would go back to being invisible.

Before he was able to follow his comrade, I grabbed his arm without setting my eyes on him. The contact sent a shock through my system. When was the last time I reached out to touch another human being? I said in a relieved and grateful tone:

"Thank you," I whispered.

Two words. But they felt like the first real words I'd spoken in years.

When I was finally able to thank him, he gave me a spark of life back. It felt like he had removed a dagger from my chest. I didn't know someone could make that feat possible. My grandma wasn't able, and my psychiatrist and all the pretenders were not capable of it.

But this boy, this stranger who had risked himself for me, had done in five minutes what months of therapy couldn't accomplish. He had reminded me that I was worth defending.

His action was genuinely made for my sake without any other plan behind it. He wasn't wearing a mask. He wasn't a charlatan. He was someone I didn't believe existed anymore. I let go of his arm so he could join his friend. Before leaving, he answered me with such sweet joyfulness in his voice:

"No problem," he replied with a smile that seemed to light up the entire world.

Then he took la poudre d'escampette, and since that day, a bond was created between us. But it was more than a bond. It was a resurrection.

I got poisoned by this world, but since that day, a flame had burned through. My body was casting away the darkness that I believed I was forever bound to. Years passed, and the newbie became my friend.

My POV

He became my anchor to what was real and good. When the nightmares came, when the trauma tried to drag me back into the darkness, I would remember this moment. Remember that someone had seen me laughing and told me it was okay.

Getting older, I eventually changed and renewed myself by learning that only the brave of heart could know true happiness. So, I decided to be bold and meet life as an equal and tackled the good and the bad as they came. After a difficult childhood, I came out from a coffin of despair, yet a scar was made to be a constant reminder of what I knew.

But scars, I learned, could be proof of healing as much as reminders of pain. And some bonds, forged in moments of pure human connection, could survive anything the world threw at them.

The bus lurches slightly, bringing me back to the present. But the warmth of that memory stays with me, a light in the storm that's coming.

"Lizzy... Lizzy... Lizzy," the bus driver calls, his voice gentle but insistent. "Time to go."

Chapter 4

The memory of Amadaniel's light fades as darker images surface. High school. Where everything I'd rebuilt came crashing down again.

My time in high school wasn't all sunshine and rainbows. It seems my personality was rubbing people the wrong way. They find me boring, noisy, annoying, and weird. I did my best to trample over their peeved eyes. I couldn't care less if they treat me like an outcast. I didn't desire to be part of that mob anyway. The set of knowledge that I acquired over the years was helpful to my growth. A mind without a body was nothing but thought loose in the air. A dream without a voice was simply the definition of a corpse.

But there's something to be said for building strength in isolation. Something about preparing for the battles that inevitably come.

Facing many challenges, I was always ready to give my best, even though my prominent strength was my intellect. I kept myself in shape through dancing and some light workouts. I won't lie, sweating was pleasant. I learned that sweating brings numerous health benefits, including boosting energy, maintaining a healthy weight, defending against various diseases and health conditions, improving mood, and, above all, the effect it has on my brain.

The physical discipline helped with the mental chaos, at least, for a while.

Walking through the halls, I was still feeling gloomy. I couldn't stop thinking about the event that occurred a few weeks back that affected the life of my best friend. Since that day, every instant of my life, I had been suffocating with guilt. I was the reason for his demise. There wasn't another way to put it. Everything happened so fast. It all begins during our lunch break. I was doing last-minute corrections to my project in my usual spot.

This is where it gets complicated, where my hunger for justice turned into something much darker.

I was inside an old white gazebo; the rails and posts were covered with wisteria. It was elegant. I was always drawn to that place; it was my new tree, but I couldn't predict during this peaceful time that a calamity was about to take place when Carl came out of the park nearby. He was walking towards me, screaming slurs, but he wasn't alone. He was accompanied by his little gang of nincompoops. I didn't understand at that time why he came at me in such an aggressive manner, but his existence alone was a nuisance for me.

Carl Brennan. Six feet of concentrated malice wrapped in designer clothes and his father's political connections.

He was a jerk who enjoyed bullying others, but regardless of that, he was popular among his peers, so no one had the guts to stop him. I couldn't put all the blame on him for his nasty behavior, knowing who raised him. His self-centered parents were making everything about them and their needs; everyone else was beneath them. On top of their bad personalities, they were both occupying positions of power in our society, with nothing to help their characters. They were despicable persons acting like they were the monarchs. Therefore, the apple didn't fall far from the tree. Growing up with that type of person will give you toxic traits.

But understanding someone's damage doesn't excuse what they choose to do with it.

Behind him, I saw his plaything, Stephanie. In that moment, I understood why he was charging at me with that much animosity. Stephanie Couture was one of my classmates and, above all, a heartless cunt. I remember earlier that day in class, I happened to humiliate her against my will. Knowing her character for judgment, she most likely felt disrespected when I corrected her on a simple question asked by the teacher. It was so trivial that I forgot how my rebuttal came out, but it sure made everyone laugh, to my biggest surprise. I didn't want to make her feel stupid, but that was the message that echoed among her peers.

Stephanie Couture. Daddy's little princess with a taste for psychological warfare and the moral compass of a broken weather vane.

I didn't understand how she could be popular and loved by many. She had an intense power trip; she manipulated friends and strangers alike, as long as she got what she wanted. She didn't give a second thought about the damage she was creating or who she hurt in the process. She was rude and egocentric behind her innocent veil. Carl enjoyed teasing me, but he never acted out of place. I had a weird connection with him; even if I found him despicable, I felt his emptiness.

Maybe that's what made what happened next so much worse. I could see the broken child underneath all that manufactured cruelty.

I didn't expect him to get involved in something this futile. There was an undesirable situation presenting itself to me through two spiteful beings. Watching them coming towards me, I needed to pack my things and flee. Facing them both meant signing my own death sentence. My heartbeat was pumping with vigorous strength; it wasn't time to think about what might happen. Carl started running towards me. I ran in the opposite direction, but Carl was already reaching the gazebo. With no effort, he climbed over the rail. I was only able to gain a few meters before he grabbed me firmly by the arm. Then he said:

"Wait. Listen before the others arrive."

Listen... listen to what? Irritated by this absurd demand, I tried to break free from his grip, but he only applied more pressure. In response, I promptly swirled a slap across his face. I managed to connect on his cheek. My sneak attack was successful. Upon the impact, he lost his grip. My only threat was stunned. My path was clear; I could feel every muscle in my legs working in harmony to maximize my swift escape. Turning around, I was ready to launch, but I couldn't even take a full step forward as he grabbed me by the hair and slammed me down to the ground.

"You're such an idiot," Carl snarled.

The words hit like a physical blow, but not because of their content. Because of the pain underneath them. The same pain I recognized in myself.

Blood was dripping from Carl's lips; he passed his tongue over his wound back and forth. He was tense. I couldn't comprehend his emotions. Something was bothering him as he spat a chunk of blood on the ground. I got up. He was looking at the gazebo as the voices of the others were getting closer. Carl turned his eyes back to me. He was about to open his mouth when Stephanie arrived and yelled:

"What the fuck are you doing!"

Carl looked back at me and gave me a hard slap across the face. I stumbled, so Carl grabbed my wrist to stop me from falling. He pulled me towards him and said in a disappointed tone, "You should have listened."

There it was again. That look. Like he was trying to warn me about something I couldn't see coming.

Dizzy from that sucker slap, my jaw was hurting. I struggled to stay on my feet; I knelt in front of him. My situation was getting worse by the second. Facing his groin, I could only think that if I managed to give him a blow hard enough in that area, I could have my ticket out of this. The rest of the gang wasn't a menace like Carl. I could outrun them with ease. Unfortunately, I couldn't get my composure to allow me to bring my plan to fruition. What could I do? What was my other possibility? Why this unnecessary violence?

The question I should have been asking about was what was coming next. About what I was about to unleash.

Carl, still holding me by the wrist, pulled me up and brought me back on my feet. Then he made long eye contact with

Stephanie, who seemed bothered by his lack of conviction, so before letting me go, he gave me a punch in the stomach that made me go back on my knees. I was in so much pain I nearly threw up as tears started falling. I felt hopeless. My arms folded. I was holding my stomach. I heard them laughing at my misfortune as they destroyed my belongings.

Her crew proceeded to shower me with mockery and insults like little trolls dancing around a campfire. Concentrating to catch my breath, I suddenly saw behind my watering eyes the white shaft of Stephanie's shoe coming straight for my face. Did I not suffer enough? With a quick reflex, I shut down my pain to quickly evade that attack. In the motions of her kick, she lost her balance and fell. From that result, I understood that she put every atom of malice behind that attack. Once again, against my will, I managed to humiliate her as her friends started laughing at her. The longer the laughter, the more punishment would come my way.

But something was building inside me. Something that felt like molten metal in my veins.

She stood up, enraged, ordering her friends to stop having fun at her expense, but they ignored her. She swiped the dirt off her butt, then she savagely grabbed me by the hair, pulling it back. I could see in her eyes rage hailing down on me like I was the source of all her pain. I could feel strands of hair preparing to leave my scalp. While looking directly in my eyes, she angrily shouted:

"You think you are funny, little bitch?"

What a sad view to witness. Her anger didn't come because of her unsuccessful attempt to cause me serious harm, but instead was fueled by the laughter of her comrades. How pathetic. Still on my knees, I held Stephanie's wrist so she couldn't pull my hair any further. Overwhelmed by the difference in strength between us, she let go of my hair and gave me a swift kick to the chest with the sole of her shoe. She stumbled backward at the impact. She started to become the clown of this interaction. Her friends enjoyed seeing her struggle to take me down. Should I use this moment to act? Should I fight back? Could I escape?

My POV

These were the questions I should have focused on. Not the darker ones beginning to whisper in my mind.

By the time I could formulate a plan, I felt a watery liquid hit my face. That trash just spat on my face. I could see it; she wanted to break me for her own guilty pleasure. While I was removing the saliva from my face, she jumped on top of me, putting me on my back, and hailed me with slaps and punches. She wasn't strong enough to inflict damage, as I easily blocked her attacks. She was mad at her failed attempt to hurt me, so she looked at her crew and ordered them to take care of me. They didn't hesitate a second to obey her demand.

After a vicious beat-down, they walked away laughing like little spawn of Satan, proud of themselves like they had carried out great deeds. Carl stayed behind for a moment after his concubine whispered something in his ear. He laid his eyes on me, then went inside the gazebo to set my stuff on fire. I was baffled by what brought this outcome. Who in their right mind would go so low? Was I wrong to think that way? I couldn't hear what Stephanie was shouting as I kept my eyes on my belongings. Getting no response from me, she tried to inflict more physical damage, but out of nowhere, in the last moment, she was stopped by Carl. They stared at each other with a murderous conviction like outlaws fighting over my fate. Then Carl said with authority:

"That's enough... let's go."

Even through my pain, I caught something in his voice. Relief? Like he'd been waiting for an excuse to stop this.

What was going on? Why now? Why? You had the power to stop this injustice, and you stood by and watched. You little piece of shit, you even participated. If it wasn't for you, I would already be gone. Why did you let that situation escalate like that? Was that pity? Should I be thankful for your intervention? I hate that feeling; it shakes me to my core. I got up and went slowly inside the gazebo. I didn't bother to put the fire out. I stood there staring at the last flames that turned my belongings to ashes. I was just contemplating in silence.

And in that silence, something poisonous began to grow.

Why do we say we are different from animals? Is it because we ignorantly think we are superior to them? Is it because they don't speak our language? Is it because we don't look alike? When you think about it, the only thing special about us is our distinct efficiency at wiping out life on Earth as we know it. Last time I checked, animals don't destroy their own home. We are prey and predator at the same time; a fish can't be anything but a fish. Even if it wanted to kill the shark, it wouldn't be able to. But us humans? We have a different window. We can adapt and change our circumstances. We have the luxury to evolve and become a shark. If we were all cannibals, imagine how low we would be on that animal kingdom chart.

I was becoming the shark. And I liked how it felt.

Then everything went quiet as I was lured to a dark, familiar place where a mix of hate, deception, and anger that I thought I had buried was emerging inside me. I didn't want to go back to my old self, but at the same time, it felt like it was the only way if I didn't want to break. Taking a deep breath, I passed my hands through my hair, pulling them back as I exhaled. I looked at the sky through the hole of this fuming gazebo. Human cruelty has no bounds. Why was I surprised? I knew that since my childhood. I worked so hard to change my beliefs about this world, but it seemed it always managed to prove to me that there would be no light in this darkened society. Too many of them wear masks. Pretenders of hope, just to trap you like an anglerfish and bring you to a deeper darkness.

I couldn't help but wonder if this life was worth living. Why stand up if people will try to keep you down? Why dream when you are too busy surviving? Will all that suffering amount to something good? Will it shape me into the best version of myself? Engulfed in my thoughts, I was brought back by a frantic voice:

"Lizzy! What happened?!" Amadaniel called out frantically.

And there he was. My anchor. My light. About to become my weapon.

I snapped out of it as I saw my friend pacing left and right in a frustrated motion. He took deep breaths to calm himself. He was battling his frustration the best he could for my sake, but seeing him like that brought me anxiety. In control of his emotions, he held me in his arms. I didn't know I needed that until I received it. It made me feel safe, such a warm body. But I was petrified by the rhythm that was playing inside his rib cage, an intense cry for blood. He delicately lifted my chin and turned it left and right to see the damage. As he examined me, he was emotionless, but his palms were sweaty. He was keeping his composure for my sake. Ashamed to have been found in that state, I kept my eyes away, holding my tears to spare him from further worries. Then he asked me with an unsettled calmness:

"Who did this, Lizzy?"

And in that moment, I made the choice that would destroy everything.

When my eyes connected with his, it paralyzed me. His eyes were filled with animosity. I didn't know who I was looking at, but staring at him like a damsel in distress didn't help. A cold breeze blew through the gazebo. The longer we kept eye contact, petrified, I became by the absence of light. I started sobbing. Facing this amount of hostility overflowing from my dear friend hurt me. I couldn't believe that those were the same eyes that brought me light in my darkest moments, but I was subjugated by the unknown. I could only let my eyes twitch in the abyss of his gaze. I didn't want to stop him. Seeing his resolve to bring those who did me wrong to their knees, I began to share his animosity. I was ready to blindly let my friend go to war for my sake. I wanted to use him as a tool of vengeance.

Because that's what trauma does, it turns love into weapons. It makes you hungry for the pain of others.

Amadaniel softly wiped away my tears. It seemed I managed to hurt him even more by reflecting his anger through my eyes. I tarnished his smile with my suffering. I kept my mouth shut and kept a smile in his presence, but by doing so, I became the type of person I despised by wearing a mask. He put his hands on my shoulders, doing whatever was humanly possible not to break, but by doing so, he squeezed my shoulders hard enough to force a grimace on my face. Aware of that, he let go of me at once, and the expression on his face changed. He looked at me with a charming smile and hugged me. Under his arms, I felt relieved and at peace. The smell of his body was sweet and brought me to a calm place. My pain was put at ease temporarily. I wanted to stay like that forever, but I couldn't ignore the infernal orchestra that was playing inside his chest. We stood in each other's arms for a moment. I knew he was waiting for me to answer his question so he could act upon my desire. I was reluctant to go down the path of vengeance, but hearing the drum of his heartbeat play with such passion, I was baited into an angry flow of thought. I went on to hug him harder before I spilled the beans.

"It was Carl and his gang."

Six words that would change everything. Six words that would take my best friend away from me forever.

I should have kept my mouth shut. With everything that unfolded that day, I wouldn't agree to let him bring my wrath on my enemies, but I was fueled by his determination. No more hiding in the corner, no more self-pity, no more weakness. He grabbed my hand, and we went back to school. As we walked, his steps were getting faster. Keeping pace with him, I couldn't stop thinking. Was I blinded by my own emotions? Was I acting with a clear conscience? Was I selfish? Was I manipulative? At the end of the day, this wasn't his battle. Why so much hesitation? Why wouldn't I rectify the wrong that had befallen me? Then we stopped. He looked down at me, and before I could say a word, he told me, "Don't worry, I got this."

Five words that should have terrified me. Instead, they thrilled me.

We entered the building; he had a look that commanded fear. His mind was already made up; he would go to the gates of hell to deliver justice. It was overwhelming. I couldn't stop smiling, pleased by his strong will, but as I smiled, a weird feeling overtook me. I couldn't recognize myself; I was craving violence to solve my problems. Could I really let him use his fists in my name? Why didn't I stop him already? Was there no other option?

But deep down, I knew there were other options. I just didn't want them anymore.

Then a loud noise of a locker door being slammed snapped me out of this guilty conscience. Looking for Carl, we walked down the hall. We arrived at a crossing; we both wondered which way to go, when I heard an irritating laugh. I saw Carl across the crowd. He was chatting and giggling with Stephanie. At that moment, something wretched crawled inside as I had a glimpse of their faces. I only felt resentment; my mind was overflowing with dark thoughts. I couldn't contain myself; I wanted them to pay more than ever. My hate for those revolting teenagers and their nonchalant attitude made my insides curdle like milk with lemon. They were the unwanted acid in what would have been otherwise delicious. The clouds of doubt that were hovering earlier disappeared in an instant.

This was the moment I became someone else. Someone who could watch violence and call it justice.

I halted his march by squeezing his hand while keeping my eyes on our targets. He turned his head to look in the direction that I pointed. Without wasting any time, he started walking towards them, bumping into a few students. He gradually picked up his pace. He didn't deviate from his path for anyone, like God himself had sent him on a mission. As he approached Carl, he started forming a fist with his graceful hand. Not far behind him, my heart rate was pumping with excitement.

I was high on the promise of violence. Drunk on the idea of watching my enemies suffer.

Amadaniel didn't even bother to announce himself. Focused like an eagle on his prey, he brought back his right arm far like an archer. As he let his arrow go straight for Carl, one of his groupies removed him from the upcoming danger. By doing so, this devastating shot kept its course towards the unaware Stephanie. She couldn't avoid it. She received the hammer of Thor straight to the face. It was a brutal, unforgiving strike. The moment she received this devastating blow, blood instantly started flowing out as her head got smashed against the wall.

No scream was heard as she was knocked out on impact. The air became deadly silent as I saw her face get crushed between the wall and the fist of her assailant. The pitiful thing didn't have time to feel any pain from this assault. With her arms lying down alongside her body, she didn't move an inch. My friend calmly removed his fist from Stephanie's face. She crumbled to the ground while sagging on the wall. It was a gory scene; her nose was an open faucet, and it was completely shattered. Looking further at her miserable state, her upper lip had a huge cut, and from that opening, I saw she was missing a few teeth. Finally, her butt reached the ground, leaving a trail of blood that came from the back of her head.

And watching this horror unfold, I felt nothing but satisfaction.

I was driven by a nefarious will; I couldn't care less. Matter of fact, I was thrilled that she was the one who took this lethal assault. There she was on the ground; I couldn't see the wound behind her head because it was covered with her heinous black hair, tainted red with the blood gushing out. I kept my eyes on her, watching her clothes dye red. I was filled with exhilaration and rapture. In that discordant orchestra, I felt something putrid wrap around my body. It was so terrifying, but at the same time so comforting. The malice that emanated from me felt good, like a warm coat. Dark thoughts begged me to surrender my soul to the most devilish deeds. I was guided by something dark, clinching my shirt, fighting the urge to inflict more damage to her lifeless body. I was angry that she passed out. Seeing her lying down like that wasn't satisfying enough. I wanted to stomp her until she became a puddle of jam under my feet. I wanted to wake her up for the sole pleasure of shouting obscenities at her. The more I kept my eyes on her, the more inhuman thoughts submerged. I couldn't contain myself anymore. As I took a few steps towards her, I wanted to end her miserable life with my bare hands by choking the life out of this bitch. At this point, it was the only sensation that would give me fulfillment. When people reach a certain point, you shouldn't invite their darkness out. We are living in an ugly world created by fear of nothing and fear of everything. Even if you find a way to defeat death, you will still be surrounded by fear. All our sins started with the simplest of things called fear.

This is where I crossed the line. Where I stopped being the victim and became something else entirely.

In the intrusion of those devilish thoughts fueled by neglected wounds, I felt strange. I felt conflicted. Did she really deserve all that loathing from me? Did justice really prevail? Was that really who I am? That strong aversion, that intense dislike for someone, couldn't be me. Seeing her in that state shouldn't bring me joy, but somehow I couldn't feel any empathy for her as I stood in front of her. I looked at the damage that my instruments of vengeance did, and I wasn't disappointed.

Suddenly, an alarming scream snapped me out of my trance. I turned around to look at Amadaniel. He was inspecting his shaking hand, covered with blood. He removed something from his hand. Then he dropped it on the floor. As I looked closely, he had removed a tooth from his hand. My friend kept his composure; I couldn't read his emotion. Something was off with both of us. We shouldn't be here. As I moved towards him to comfort him, he looked at me and gave me a heart-warming smile. I could only respond with a smile of my own, but somehow, I felt uneasy. I didn't want to lose him. While he removed another canine from his hand, Carl charged at him. He easily avoided him, then he flicked the tooth at Carl's face. Seeing him attacking with blind rage, I could see the pain and the anger that Carl was expressing, and it disgusted me, rubbing me the wrong way.

Even watching Carl's genuine anguish, all I felt was satisfaction.

How could he express that type of emotion if, a few minutes ago, he treated me like trash, laughing while he was doing his evil deeds with his precious imp? How could he stand there with resentment in his eyes? How many people did he make suffer without remorse? Why should I feel pity for him? Even by the display of his desolation, he was still a rag. If you know the strength of pain, why inflict it on others? What do you gain from that? He deserved to suffer for all he did. How could I let myself enter that wheel of hate? A never-ending cycle that corrupts the core of your person. I was sinking in a place where the light didn't shine on the lost souls, a road filled with loneliness and sadness, but it was too late for me. I couldn't stop as I let my cynical thoughts have the best of me. I wanted to see him crumble under the weight of his karma. I wanted to see him suffer until I was satisfied. It was a true delight to see Carl in that state of pain; it was like a serenade in my ears.

Carl charged with a hard series of punches. He was putting all his emotions behind those fists, giving Amadaniel many good hits, but it wasn't enough to bring my titan down. He finally brought up his guard and blocked Carl's next attack with ease and countered with a mean right hook that sent Carl flying into the lockers. Carl was clearly no match for him, making me question if he let Carl lash out at him on purpose. I couldn't give a care in the world to be bothered with that assumption. I was consumed by vengeance; the empathy I felt was just a default reflection of my personality. I had tunnel vision; seeing Carl struggle only brought me animation. I wanted to see him on his knees. I wanted his light to be snuffed out; I desired nothing else than the guillotine.

Carl quickly went back on his feet and kept his distance as I saw fear devouring him. He was bleeding abundantly from his mouth, standing there like a beaten dog looking for a way to save his ass. Then out of nowhere, Carl's goons came to his aid. My warrior was outnumbered four to one. Carl was the leader of the gang, but Aramus was easily the strongest in his group. He finished third in the national boxing event last year but sustained an injury last month. Mathias was the weakest among them. He was tall and skinny but quick on his feet, and finally, Lindor. He was an odd one. He was more like a sheep with no future who followed the crew in their devious acts.

They simultaneously charged, but my friend managed to defend himself, mostly by avoiding Aramus's punches. He managed to distance himself from arms' way, but the space to maneuver freely had become restrained by the number of students that gathered around this brouhaha, forming a thick wall around us. Irritated not to have the advantage in this handicap match, they started to get dirtier with their assault. My friend couldn't keep up with that type of assault. He received a punch in the gut that brought him down on one knee. To his disadvantage, his aggressors took a moment to taunt him. Carl joined them as they held both arms of Amadaniel. Mathias encouraged Carl to give the final blow. In a position of power and control, his cockiness reappeared. He took a few steps back and dashed toward his prey, giving him a flying knee straight to his face.

I couldn't believe he managed to receive this violent blow without serious injury. Standing a few meters away, I didn't move an inch. How could I be this useless? Did I really expect no rebuttal to this declaration of war? How could I be so pathetic? Didn't I choose violence to solve my issues? Why was I surprised? I knew the risk. This wasn't the time to be a coward. THINK! LIZZY! THINK! But nothing came up. I couldn't come up with something. Fear was making me spiral into deeper negative thoughts. I was weak. I was destined to be an eternal victim. I disconnected myself from what was happening, swallowing myself in self-pity. I wanted to run, but I couldn't abandon someone who was fighting my demons. I couldn't dispose of him like that. I wouldn't be able to forgive myself for this act of betrayal. I needed to reverse the situation, and standing there, drowning in my own guilt, won't make a thing budge.

Everything was blowing back to my face. He was getting roughly handled because of my hunger for vengeance. There I was, cowardly from my actions; my momentary pleasure was bringing me more pain than anything else. I could feel a void open where guilt makes you more rotten and less healthy. Carl asked his crew to lift him so he could go at it one more time. Carl, ready to charge again. I couldn't be this useless. I rushed towards him, screaming with all the air available in my lungs:

"Stop!" I screamed with everything I had.

To my great surprise, I managed to stop Carl. All eyes on me. Carl gave me the same distressful looks that he had at the gazebo. Was I the only one able to see it? Then a shout from Mathias snapped both of us from this strange vibe.

"Hey, what the fuck are you doing?!" Mathias yelled.

That moment allowed Amadaniel to set himself free. He surprised Aramus with a sting to the chin, putting him out of combat. The crowd was in for quite a show. By the time the rest of the gang could react, the next counterattack was already in motion as he grabbed Mathias by his shirt and threw him as hard as he could towards Lindor, sending them both flying. Carl took a few steps back. Amadaniel struggled to stay up. Outraged by this rebuttal, Carl grabbed an extinguisher and charged with murderous intention towards Amadaniel. What should I do? Unable to act, I stood there watching Carl arrive with a full extension of his arm upward, solidifying both his feet on the floor, ready to deliver a devastating blow. Responsible for this upcoming mess, I couldn't steer my eyes from this. It seemed my brain wanted to perpetually keep this upcoming gruesome scenery of my biggest debacle trapped in my head. Like the main villain of a story, my desires led me to more misery. My emotions got the best of me. To what end? I still lose, no matter the path I chose. If only I could exchange places with him.

Then, when all hope was lost, a valiant shout surged from the crowd. It was Eddy, a beast like no other, making an impressive entrance. He was a well-built young man. On top of this, he was an ally to my combatant. He tackled Carl to the ground, then lifted him and gave him a strong blow directly in the stomach. Eddy lifted Carl's head and gave him a hard headbutt, then finished his combo by grabbing him by the shoulders to throw him away like a bag of potatoes.

Lindor and Mathias went to the aid of their friend by charging towards Eddy. He didn't seem bothered by this, as he welcomed Mathias with a right hook directly on the chin that made him stumble backward. He swiftly changed his stance to block the strike of Lindor. After a successful maneuver, he gave one mean kick to Lindor's privates. Seeing Mathias grab the extinguisher, he rushed to him and gave him a hard push that sent him flying into the crowd. From that, a massive brawl started. The hall became a real nut house. Personnel and security guards were charging into the midst of those hormonal teenagers to put out the fire. In the wave of this chaos, my gladiator fled the warzone, so I decided to do the same. Making my way out of this ruckus, I lost sight of Amadaniel. Far from this brawl, I managed to recollect myself. The bell rang to announce that the lunch break was over. I couldn't find him before returning to class.

The gossip was spreading all over the place about the event that occurred. Curious, I laid my ears to some of those feeds. I heard that Stephanie had been escorted to an ambulance. People were talking about the presence of police officers in the school. I made a quick calculation; someone went to the hospital, and the police officers were showing up. Things didn't sound good; I needed to find him, so I excused myself from class to go find him. Walking in the corridor, I saw him. Seeing him without handcuffs appeased me and brought a smile. I rushed towards him unnoticed; I was charmed by those broad shoulders that could carry the weight of the earth in the name of justice. He was a unique individual. Making my dark thoughts fade away without any effort, when I finally reached the perfect distance, I jumped on his back in laughter, glad to have him around my arms. Then I whispered, reassured, "I got you."

He just stood there and didn't say a word. He gently lowered himself so I could get down. The atmosphere was strange; I was getting anxious. As I stepped down, he turned around to face me and hugged me. The air was somber. I didn't need to be a genius to see something bad had happened, but still, I needed to hear it from him. I nervously asked, "What's wrong?"

He kept me under his arms and told me in a calm voice.

"Listen... I made a mistake."

The words that would shatter my world.

My heart started stomping. I didn't like how this conversation was starting. I slowly backed my head up, looked at him with worries stamped all over my face. He smiled at me, trying to soothe my stress, and proceeded with the same calm voice. He started to explain what was going on.

"The outcome of my actions was well... unexpected."

Defeated, I stood there heartbroken. Every word that was coming through his mouth had been recorded; not even a bomb could interrupt my concentration to the point I would stop my heartbeat, so I couldn't miss one decibel. I was fooled by an optimistic state of mind, a blind desire to predict what seemed a preposterous positive outcome. He gently breaks off our embrace and keeps talking. I couldn't comprehend his emotion; he seemed empty but pleased at the same time. How come? Did I miss something? Was there something I didn't know? I looked at him straight in the eyes, and they were giving me a heartfelt "Adieu". Baffled by what was going on, my emotions went off the charts. Sadness, anger, hate, pain, frustration, rage, deception; I was overwhelmed by guilt. How could I have been so useless? How didn't I see that my beacon was torn? I felt a burning sensation rushing inside me, making my heart play the drum of the fallen. His words became echoes as the hymn kept playing louder. My entire body was burning, lacing my veins and creeping up my spine. My chest was hurting; I wanted to rip my heart from my chest with my bare hands and give it to him to show him how deeply sorry I was. He then finished with a downhearted voice:

"I need to face the consequences."

The final blow. The moment I realized I had destroyed the only pure thing in my life.

My POV

I was intoxicated with negative emotions. The acidity of it was living in my stomach, waiting to be spat out of my mouth in foul and vulgar ways. I wasn't just going to say them; I was about to screech them with every ounce of breath that dwelled in my lungs. I couldn't contain myself anymore as I lashed out my anger in denial of this insufferable explanation, "THAT PILE OF SHIT and his low-life underlings hurt me more than once... NOTHING! NOTHING! was ever done to stop them. They could have prevented all of that before it could reach that size, but they didn't. THEY ALL LEFT ME ALONE!"

I couldn't hold it anymore as tears were falling while I was evacuating my pain. He was the only one who could understand me. He didn't try to stop me, correct me, or lift me; he just listened to my pain. The more I spoke, the harder it became for me to make a coherent sentence as I mumbled my words. If I could tear their flesh apart with my teeth, I would, just to hear them implore me to stop and beg for forgiveness. My hatred for them only grew stronger. They could literally die in front of me, and I wouldn't share a thought for them. They were pure trash of humanity. Lashing out a rain of insane enmity made me ill. My blood pumping in my head made me dizzy. I was disoriented. Exposing signals of distress, he wrapped me around his arms once more and put my head to rest on his chest. The tension went down as I took a moment to breathe. In a broken voice, I told him, "That punch doesn't even equal what they put me through."

After this explosion of emotions, I couldn't believe how calm his heartbeat was. How could he be unshaken by this tsunami of fury? Was he staying strong for me? Or maybe he was done feeling pity for me? Why couldn't I feel turmoil in his heartbeat? With what I made him do for my sake, I literally brought him to his downfall, yet I felt no hostility. Spiraling in my despair, his grip became tighter, and he told me in a guilty voice, "I'm sorry, Lili."

What could you have done? I was the one hiding my pain behind a mask, avoiding letting my torment brush on you. My stress, my fear, my own tribulations were not meant to be all carried by him. I couldn't rely on him every time I get stomped on. I just couldn't use him like that, basing our relationship on that sole purpose. He gave me so much already while I had so little to give. It hurt me to be the source of his troubles. I couldn't bear my own self. I couldn't even ask him for forgiveness. What could I do? What should I do? Darkness awaited me once more. I would be a boat without an anchor. I needed to concentrate on the present situation and find a solution. It wasn't the time to let clouds of negativity weaken me more. I needed to become his beacon, help him more than ever. Maybe the principal could help if I explained to him how it all came to fruition. He took a deep breath, stepped back while holding both of my hands, and gave me a gentle smile full of kindness and purity. The same one that enlightened me when we were kids, and told me, "Lili, none of that's your fault."

The lie that broke my heart. Because we both knew it wasn't true.

How could he look me in the eyes and tell me that bullshit? In that story, I was the villain hidden behind the curtain, letting my minions do my hard bidding. Then I heard an irritated voice shout, "They are waiting!" the security guard called out impatiently.

Irked by his presence, he let go of my hands. He didn't even glance at me as he turned around without adding another word and left. I couldn't let this be our last interaction. I couldn't just stand there like a widow. The door of the hall shut, letting the echoes of regret fill the room. I ran to join him. There I was, standing on top of the stairs; I didn't even know what to tell him. Sorry, wouldn't cut it. He went inside a patrol car. He was sitting with his head down; this foreboding look struck me. Should I fight the officer? Should I plead his innocence to the officer? I needed to be the one to blame for his actions. I should be the one sitting in the backseat of this police patrol. What could I do to turn the tables in my favor? While being everything but helpful, I stood there watching the car roll away, hoping for Amadaniel to look at me one more time or at least tell me what to do. There was an urgency to act now. I turned around and made a run towards the principal's office. I went past the secretary without even giving her the chance to react or stop my intrusion. I burst into the office, driven by so much fervent emotion, and yet my mind was blank of solutions to change this series of events.

Once inside, I was welcomed by the most repugnant creatures on the face of the Earth. Carl was sitting in the office. It was still delightful to see him bruised up, but I wished he had received Stephanie's fate. The more I looked at him, the more my thoughts were vile. There wasn't any place for remorse, especially for that cockroach. I wanted to paint the walls red with his guts while joyfully listening to the symphony of his agony. It would have been a fine tune, exquisite like fine wine. He didn't lay an eye on me and abruptly exited. Absorbed by my vengeful thoughts, I was brought back in check by Robert Fisher, our principal, as he spoke to me, "Explain yourself, Miss Bonaventure!"

Standing in the entrance of the room, I didn't respond to the call. The principal, sitting in his chair, removed his glasses and took a cloth from his drawer to clean them. He let go of a disappointing sigh before cleaning his glasses. Then he asked me, "What's the meaning of this intrusion?"

I didn't want to be hasty with my words, so I clenched my fists hard enough to help me concentrate and be able to respond appropriately to Mr. Fisher. "I need to talk with you."

The principal put on his glasses and leaned forward with both elbows on his desk. He sat there quietly with his hands tangled close to his mouth. He looked at me, then with a hand gesture, invited me to sit down. I needed to give a flawless presentation to save a kind and compassionate soul who made a terrible mistake for an unworthy person. I couldn't back down now. Without wasting another second, I went straight forward and explained to him the cause of this brutal story. I didn't fight enough, and by doing so, I let myself become a victim of bullies. After hearing what I had to say, he looked at me, concerned.

"Why didn't you come to me?" he asked.

I looked at him with despair in my eyes.

"I have been let down by adults since my childhood. Before your arrival, my situation wasn't taken seriously. They were just putting patches on a deeper wound and gave my aggressors ammunition to inflict me greater pain each time."

He was bothered to learn all this. He cracked his knuckles. Then he responded:

"Sorry to hear that, but I could have fixed this problem of yours before it got out of hand."

So much certainty in his voice. It seemed there was no lie in what he was saying, but at the same time, I didn't think he understood the task that was in front of him. He was just behaving like any adult would in his position. I wasn't a fool; he was just showering me with lies with that make-believe asset. We both knew what he was suggesting only meant career suicide. Why would he sacrifice what he worked hard to achieve for some stranger? Either way, it was too late. The deeds were already done. What might have happened was just echoes that were trapped in the past. Sitting there, I realized how I failed lamentably; all that talk was for nothing. My testimony was just air in an empty room. Even though Mr. Robert Fisher changed the mentality of this establishment in an effective way, in the end, there wasn't much he could do outside of those four walls. I wanted to crawl into a corner and erase myself from this world. No matter what I tried to do, it always amounted to nothing. Looking down at my clenched fists, desperately hiding my frustration and guilt by knowing I ruined the life of the one person who brought me light in this blind and melancholy world, where the weak drown in silent, killing me softly. The principal got up and went to the counter near the entrance of his office, where he poured himself a glass of coffee, accompanied by a resonating silence. Stirring his coffee, he went to sit back at his desk, then looked at me.

"Miss Stephanie Couture went to the hospital with severe injuries to the head. The young man's assaults on a fellow student of that intensity of bloodshed must be met with consequences that are beyond my reach."

My POV

The principal took a brief pause, blew on his hot drink before taking a sip. What was I doing? None of that was productive. I knew the situation was hopeless the moment Amadaniel entered the police car. Sitting there, watching my feeble hands, I understood it was pointless for me to seek further help. There was nothing for me to hope. I got up. I apologized for my intrusion and left the room without saying a word. I was blinded by a worthless emotion that brought me nothing more than more pain in the end. The day went on, but mine stopped the moment Amadaniel had been taken into custody.

Chapter 5

Another memory surfaces, darker than the ones before. This is where everything I built with Amadaniel's help began to crumble. Where I learned that losing someone you love doesn't just leave you empty, it transforms you into something else entirely.

The atmosphere at school was grim. I was thinking about the letter and realized I hadn't seen Carl since we last crossed paths in the principal's office. Since the event, I hadn't smiled once. I lost all contact with Amadaniel; I couldn't find any information about what was going on with him. I went to his place, but his parents welcomed me with a cold shoulder. They didn't dare to utter a word to me besides letting me know I was scum. My world was in shambles. I was on my own with this heavy, humid fog of depression that was slowly choking me. The conversation that was going around school was that Stephanie was in a coma. With the severity of the assault, she received a permanent brain injury. They said that the left part of her body was paralyzed.

The news should have filled me with regret. Instead, all I felt was a hollow satisfaction that made me hate myself even more.

Today, the class was half empty; it seemed that the announcement of the upcoming storm had everyone on edge. The last time something of that magnitude happened was when I lost my parents. On my desk, I was looking through the window, gazing at nothing. The gloomy weather that was presented to me made me melancholy. The clumsy sky was slowly bringing me unwanted memories. Was I cursed to roam in the darkness? I lost everyone dear to me; I was always in the front row when they left. I was a walking plague.

"Lizzy, es-ce que ça va? Li... zzy?" the French teacher called.

Her voice seemed to come from far away, like an echo in a tunnel.

My POV

I was doomed. How could I escape this? Was there a way to escape? Was I trapped? Argh! I hated my state of mind.

"Madame Bonadventure!" she called more sharply.

I snapped out of it and looked at her. She looked at me, concerned, and bent down and whispered:

"You don't look well, Lili," she whispered.

Even her kindness felt like an intrusion. I didn't deserve concern. I didn't deserve anything.

"Non tout va bien, j'étais juste dans la lune," I replied with a smile.

The lie came so easily. I was becoming an expert at wearing masks.

She acknowledged my statement and pursued her course, but to be honest, I needed help. Alone in the middle of the ocean, I was drifting to nowhere, but regardless of this emotion, I felt like I didn't deserve to ask for it. I was so wrapped in my own pain that I forgot today was the birthday of my father. I wished he were there. My grandmother told me he was a loving and kind person. He was very soft-hearted, ready to help anyone in need in whatever way he could. His name was François Bonadventure, born and raised in France in a small village. He traveled a lot, guided by the love of different art around the globe. Grandma also told me; he didn't want to build a family for fear of being forced to stop his adventures. My father had everything to please, but I was quite sure Grand-maman was adding more than she should. Nonetheless, it was nice to remember him like that. Grand-maman told me everything came to a stop when something colossal happened, and her name was Eliza Hayes, my mom. She was a redhead; her hair looked exactly like mine. Every time I looked at myself, I saw her, the burnt orange sunset over the bay. It was warm, and it tumbled over her shoulders like rusty water. I had a lot of her traits. Watching pictures of her when she was a teenager always made me blush, but I couldn't match her beauty. She was a scientist. She was always reading something; her knowledge was vast. She always seemed at peace when she was reading. She enjoyed the challenges of life even. She was a fierce woman, giving her best in everything she put her mind to. My parents met at an event that was held in my mom's city.

These memories felt like looking at someone else's life. A life where people were whole and happy and didn't destroy everything they touched.

My time with them was brief, as they both died in a car crash. Everything happened in an instant during a stormy night. The wind was strong, and the rain was falling heavily. The sky was dark; the thunders were loud, unleashing monstrous roaring sounds. My mom was about to give birth to my little brother. My little brother wasn't due yet. She was in trouble because of her medical condition; it was vital for her to give birth in the hospital, but we weren't that lucky. The weather made it impossible for the emergency services to deploy to us. My parents had no choice but to take on the storm. That night, my mom was howling in agony, making me tremble in fear. Everything was so loud. Even with my hands on my ears, I couldn't cancel out the cacophony that was surrounding me. Driving us into this chaotic, weathered darkness, my dad was doing everything in his power to aid my mom and reassure me. The rain was smashing down with a relentless rhythm. Thunder was illuminating the sky. At the speed we were going, he handled it like a champ, but my mom's health was becoming worse by the second. Despite the odds, everything was going in our favor. My dad was phenomenal. He was taking curves with precision. He was focused like an eagle. I felt like nothing could stop us, but then my dad made a quick maneuver to avoid an obstacle on the road. He lost control and went into a precipice, flipping multiple times. Each barrel roll brought a thunderous clap. The rain was hailing on the car like it wanted to rip it apart. Then total silence.

And in that silence, everything I was supposed to become died with them.

After this horrific event, you might already guess, I had many nights' terrors. I was disconnected from the world. I muted myself. My parents had made my grandmother my legal guardian. My grandma, Arielle Bonaventure, really took good care of me. She was the nicest person I knew. When she spoke about my parents, it always brought me butterflies in my stomach. Every day, she was walking long distances. She could appear drowsy in her movements on the way home, but she enjoyed the exercise. In the winter, her knees were getting slightly inflamed from the cold, but it didn't stop her. I had never seen her wear shabby clothes; they were always clean and fresh. She had the most angelic smile. Even though her voice could appear feeble at times, she was still able to guide me. Sometimes her eyes could appear milky when she was tired, but they were still gleaming with life.

When I was a teen, her health was degrading. She had Alzheimer's. I didn't suspect anything. She did her best to manage her condition so I wouldn't be taken away from her. I took part in her charade and covered for her when pieces of her mind were giving up. Over the years, it started to become harder for us to play this act. The sickness was affecting her more viciously than expected. I kept my mouth shut and tried to manage, but it made me lonelier. I had no one to reach out to. I needed to find a way to change my mind. My usual tricks didn't work; I was burned physically and mentally.

By the time she forgot my name, I was already learning how to disappear inside myself. How to build walls that nothing could breach.

The bell rang; it was an exhausting day even though I didn't do anything but think. I went to the bathroom to splash some water on my face. While in there, I heard giggles in the stall behind me. There were two people inside. I lay an ear to their conversation. One of them was describing her latest sexual encounter. I just stood there giving an attentive ear. Something inside me was tingling as I kept listening like a pervert to every detail. She sounded happy, free, and in control. I felt ashamed to wish to receive such enjoyment. The girls came out; one of them came up next to me. I didn't dare to lay an eye on her. Standing awkwardly in front of the sink, she said to me, "Aren't you going to wash your hands?" she asked.

Her voice had this teasing quality that made my skin flush.

I didn't even respond to her. I quickly opened the faucet. Then I heard her giggle. I kept washing my hands, hoping she would just walk away, but instead, she closed my faucet, laid her lips next to my ear, and with an amused tone said:

"Did you hear my story?" she whispered.

The question sent electricity down my spine. She knew. She knew I'd been listening, and she didn't care.

I replied by pleading ignorance.

"No, I just arrived," I replied.

She got closer to my ear. "Your nipples are telling me otherwise," she said with a smirk.

Heat flooded through me. Shame and excitement twisted together in my stomach.

I immediately looked down at my shirt.

"Aren't you the cutest?" she purred.

My body was getting hot. I couldn't move. She aroused me with her unconventional approach. I couldn't believe the amount of excitement that was rushing through me. What was wrong with me? I should just walk away. Was she flirting with me? To what end? In all those questions, the one that resonated above all was why did it feel so good? Lost in my thoughts, she used that moment to softly kiss me on the neck. I let a pleased moan echo in this empty restroom. She grabbed me by the hands to face her.

"Don't be shy," she coaxed.

This girl, this stranger, was offering me something I'd never even known I wanted.

I stood there, swallowing my own saliva. She brought her lips closer to mine. Eyes wide open, I didn't move a muscle. I didn't even know what she looked like, yet I didn't deny her approach. I was pulled by a strong sexual urge that was blazing through my entire body. I wanted her lips to connect with mine so badly. I wanted to feel something other than despair, loneliness, guilt, and the armor of failure. Like a fairy tale, I wished that kiss would put my troubled mind at ease. Her hand was soft. The more the tension reached its climax, the more I squeezed her hand. Then the door of the bathroom was slammed open. Her friend entered the room and shouted, "Hey, we don't have all day!"

The spell shattered like glass.

She moved her head to my ear and softly told me in a disappointed voice, "Sorry, *Bella*. I don't like to be rushed."

Then she just left the room, leaving me baffled by what had occurred. I tried to keep my composure, but the harder I tried, the more aroused I got. Facing the mirror, I looked at my body. I needed to change my mindset. I splashed some water on my face, thinking it would make me calm. It was a laughable illusion. My desire just kept raging on. I felt conflicted by my needs, my desires, my inexperience. Should I claim ownership of my sexuality? How should I do that? Should I feel ashamed? It was my body at the end of the day. No? I never had such intense urges.

But maybe that was exactly what I needed. Something to drown out the guilt and the grief. Something that was mine and mine alone.

I was thinking about how it would be delectable if I acted on those impulses, reached the realm of unknown pleasure. The thoughts of a full-blown orgasm weren't helping me to keep my composure. I was rubbing my legs together, but I was only stimulating myself. I started caressing my soft skin. Just picturing my encounter made me tingle down to my toes. Such a toxic combination of fantasy, lust, and physical sensation. At that moment, I knew what I would do when I got home. I arrived at my stop. I could see the sky darkening; the wind was starting to blow, making the leaves rattle slowly. It seemed the storm would hit us a bit sooner. To save time, I took my usual shortcut. A few droplets started falling, so I began to jog down the old road filled with numerous obstacles that I avoided effortlessly. I saw the bridge. Keeping a steady pace, I crossed it. From there, I could see the houses. I reached my home before I could say Pneumonoultramicroscopicsilicovolcanoconiosis. I didn't spend a second in the entrance. I quickly got naked and ran to the bathroom to prepare a bath. I opened the window; black clouds sprawled across the sky. The scent of rain was dark and heady but brought a sweet, natural aroma into the room. After the preparation was done, I went inside my warm bath.

This would be mine. This moment, this feeling, this choice, finally, something that belonged only to me.

Water enveloped my body. I tenderly caressed my body. I felt so good. My stomach fluttered with nervous butterflies. My breath caught in my chest as my fingers ventured down. I closed my eyes, circled my fingertips around my clit, and a shaky breath stuttered across my lips. My flesh felt hot and heavy under my hand, and I cupped myself, letting my fingers slip between the folds of my sex. The weight of my desire became like an electric current. My lungs seized; my limbs quivered. I opened my eyes. A soft groan escaped. I continued to move my hand towards my vagina. A perverse thrill shot through me, and I shivered. Without relenting, I lifted my leg across the edge of the bath and stretched my legs wider so I could rub and massage my overheated pussy lips. My pussy was a teasing welcome of relief. I slid my fingers down my clit, letting them delve inside, burying them between my precious pink lips. I took my time to explore it.

It was a sweet pleasure. As the sound of water clapping between my hands made my mind frolic, my senses all tingled and came together so gloriously. My head fell back. Biting my lips, I continued to thrust my hand back and forward, rubbing my insides with such devotion. I moved my hips in ways that stimulated my clitoris, giving me immense pleasure.

Outside, a stillness falls and, in the silence, comes a low crackle of thunder, rolling. I parted my thighs further, letting my fingers wander deeper. My thighs tensed; I planted my shoulders firmly against the bath with my hips up. I was in full control of my body. I felt every fiber of my body connect to give me a sensational orgasm. My head fell back. My chest rose then fell rhythmically as I jerked my body in passionate and tender strokes, making the water overflow out of the bath. My nipples had never been that hard. I couldn't help myself as I began to thrust faster. Seeing light at the end of the tunnel, I knew I was on the edge of climax.

This was mine. This pleasure, this power over my own body, this moment where nothing else existed but sensation.

That moment was mine and mine alone to sink into this lechery. A bath of my own endorphins was just what I needed. Stroking my fingers deeper and deeper, the wind opened the window violently. I kept going. I could smell the upcoming heavy downpour. Water kept splashing out of the bath. I moaned in euphoria as the downpour began like no precedent. Reaching the seventh heaven, a loud thunder crackled near the house. The room was illuminated by a radiant light, casting no shadow. Then everything went dark.

In that darkness, I realized something had shifted. I was no longer just the girl who lost everything. I was becoming someone who could take what I wanted, feel what I chose to feel. The transformation Amadaniel's arrest had started was accelerating, and I wasn't sure I wanted to stop it.

The storm outside mirrors the one in this memory. I touch the window, feeling the vibrations of thunder, and I know that night changed me forever. Not just because I discovered my sexuality, but because I learned I could find power in the darkest moments. That realization would shape everything that came after.

Chapter 6

This sexual awakening dissolves into something else entirely. Something that should have been beautiful but became another kind of darkness.

In total darkness, I stood up and went to the window. I took a deep breath and inhaled the natural freshness inside my lungs to calm my nerves. I laid my eyes outside; I could see a tree snapped in two by this tremendous thunder. My mental state under control, I turned around to go to my room, but fear petrified me. In front of me, there was an individual standing. Everything went silent. I didn't scream; I didn't even move a muscle. I held my breath to eliminate every trace of my presence. Then the stranger said with an enlivened voice, "Breathe, Lizzy."

His voice was like warm honey, but there was something underneath it that I couldn't place. Something that should have warned me.

What in the blue hell? How did he know my name? I was done for; there was no escape besides the window. I slowly stepped back toward the window. Then a strong wind blew, closing the window, startling me. Then he spoke to me in a reassuring tone, using once more my name like we were good old buddies.

"Lizzy, it's okay. Don't be afraid."

"Who the fuck are you?" I demanded.

I should have been terrified. Any rational person would have been. But something about his presence was already working on me, dulling my instincts.

Before he could answer, the light went back on. The first glimpse I had of him shattered every logical thought. I was soothed by his presence. Was it lust? He had a smile that put me at ease from any malicious thoughts. My fear faded away like dust in the wind. The person standing in front of me came straight from a fable. He had soft brown skin, dreadlocks with golden and silver rings at random locations, and dark eyes that were making me weak in the knees. I could feel that he had the heart of a lion and the soul of an angel. He was tall with a slim, muscular body. His face was perfectly symmetrical. He had this African heritage glowing from him. In any given circumstance, an encounter like that should be terrifying, but the aura of this stranger was beyond my comprehension. In that moment, his entire existence was making my heart pound vigorously. He then went ahead and introduced himself.

"My name is Hadraniel, but you can call me Daniel."

Even his name sounded like salvation. Like something divine had finally come to rescue me from all the darkness.

Still baffled by what was going on, I took a deep breath.

"Okay... okay, Daniel, what are you doing in my bathroom?"

"You called me."

Astonished by his answer, I responded:

"Called you?!? I don't even know you."

He didn't say a word, then he approached me. Even though I was still on guard, I had no desire to flee or fight. He lifted my chin up, then smiled at me.

"I'm sorry that I showed myself unannounced. If you desire me to leave, I will."

But I didn't want him to leave. Even then, some part of me knew I was already lost.

I didn't respond. I was drawn to him; looking deep into his eyes, I was seduced by what he wanted to offer me. By the proximity of our bodies, I could feel that he wanted to spoil me with nothing but love. He stood there, letting me know that he would build a path where only tears of joy would grace my skin. A path where pain would be nonexistent.

"I'm here for you," he said.

He leaned forward, then kissed me on the lips. I felt unconditional love seizing my entire body; the softness of his lips soothed me. His warm breath, spiced with the scent and crisp sweetness of ambrosia, rushed across my senses and threatened to steal my own breath. Eyes were said to be the doorway to the soul. So, I would say the lips were the passageway to the mind. Lips react to the mind's thoughts in so many ways. They can show happiness with a smile, express their thoughts and feelings, but a kiss? Well, the kiss was highly underrated. It said many things that were difficult or impossible to put into words, but at this moment, all my doubts, all my questioning, were washed away. At this moment, I was over the moon to be in his presence. I had found my missing link. I caressed his face with tears of joy, like I had found my long-lost lover. Wiping my tears away, he leaned forward to passionately kiss me once more. My entire body was engulfed in hot sexual tension; I couldn't hold myself together as I let my naughty thoughts guide me. I sensually whispered, "I trust you."

Should I have let myself trust someone with that much ease?

He grabbed me by the hips with a firm yet gentle grip and lifted me out of the room. My legs wrapped around him, and we entered my bedroom. He gently put me down in front of my bed. We stared at each other like we had reunited after a century; it was inconceivable. He passed his hand through my hair, watching it tumble as he released it. Then his hand moved down my cheekbones to my lips. Kneeling on top of me, the fervent kissing started again. We were in perfect sync. Every kiss was delivered with raw intensity; my heart rate went faster. I felt his fingers playing around my most intimate places. Our tongues entwined in our kisses, his fingertips were electric. They must have been, for wherever they touched my skin, it tingled in a frenzy of static. Then he stopped kissing me, brought his lips to my nipples, and sucked on them while still playing at the entrance to my vagina. Holding his head down, forcing him to suck me dry, that delicious sensation traveling all over my body was delightful. Kissing me tenderly all the way down to my center, he started licking the surrounding area. Then, with his mouth wide open, he covered my vagina before inserting his luscious tongue inside, making my pussy drip even more. He knew how to hit the right spot, making me squeeze the sheets as my back arched so he could taste every drop of my wet pussy. It felt like my soul was about to leave my body. I moaned and moaned without restraint. My body had a temporary paralysis toward this newfound pleasure. Letting my juices squirt on his face like a firehose, I wanted more. I wanted to go further. Everything was simple; he was mine, and I was his. I felt the tip of his cock gently rubbing on my vulva. The excitement was at its highest. Ready to give him my virginity, I gave him my consent.

"Take me away."

"As you wish."

And with those words, I surrendered completely to something I thought was love.

Then he slowly made his way in. I could feel my vulva being stretched by his hardness, but against everything I had read and seen, it wasn't painful at all. He continued to penetrate me with grace. The wetness of my pussy was overwhelming. He was regulating my breathing with every thrust, hearing my moans timed to his body. Both of us moved in an intoxicated dance of limbs, moving back and forward. I burst, letting out a loud moan. He kept going in and out. I was trembling with pleasure, moving my hips like a snake. I ground on his dick faster. I couldn't be stopped. I didn't want to stop. The room was hot; the bed and everyone on it was showered by my juices. Breathing heavily, I held my head, trying to keep my composure from this thrill, assimilating all those feelings. We kept at it. He started pounding with more desire; the thrusts didn't slow down even when I felt his cum filling my insides. I kept grinding, making his body shake uncontrollably. The sweet noise of our cum mixing, splattering all over us, was delightful. I couldn't help it as I rode faster to burst once more before his stiff rod lay to rest. It was wet and sticky all over the place. We were both exhausted. He lay next to me. Regardless of our state, we tangled. I started to fall asleep as he played with my hair gently without saying a word. I closed my eyes with my head lying on his chest.

That night, I thought I had found paradise.

I woke up; my head was buzzing. I looked around; there was no one in the room. The house was quiet. Maybe I was dreaming about my encounter last night, but it couldn't be true because it was so vivid. I went downstairs. I could smell one of my favorite breakfasts that my grandma used to make. I arrived in the kitchen; there was no one. I looked at the table; a plate was set. I sat down and began to eat. There was a note on the table, but I couldn't understand the handwriting.

Intoxicated by love, I didn't pay attention to the sign and went straight to fill my empty stomach.

I finished school. I arrived home, and there he was, waiting for me at the porch. He received me by giving me a hug. I felt comfort in his arms. Everything was perfect. I couldn't ask for more. I was showered with love. As time passed, I would wait eagerly for his visits. I was addicted to his voice. I would get anxious if I didn't talk to him. He was my artificial oxygen tank. Every time I laid eyes on him, I felt blessed. I knew that if he wanted to, he could have someone better than me, less damaged and more worthy. Someone with a smaller waist, blonde hair, more self-confidence, not shy, not geeky. But apparently, his love for me had no equal. His desires for me were bigger than lust. He made me realize that sex and love were two different things. Sex was a simple physical act, so simple that even animals do it. But lovemaking was a complex expression of love. It was a desire to communicate the affection, the desire you have for the other person, with a physical interaction where both are one. It lets you express it in the form of a deep-felt connection with your significant other. I remembered there was a time when girls said that they viewed giving someone their virginity as like giving boys an incredibly special gift. Because of this, they often expected something in return, such as increased emotional intimacy with their partners. However, they often felt disempowered because of this; they often didn't feel like they received what they expected in return. But now, most of them don't have this mentality or this need. As women, we progressed a lot in a world of men, but it seemed that we were slowly losing our way in different aspects of our lives. We could do as we pleased, but we shouldn't forget that all actions have consequences. Let's not become the clowns of the circus when we could all enjoy a good show. Was I old-fashioned or delusional?

Love had cast a fog so strong that common sense couldn't prevail.

Daniel was everything that I always wished for. He was a ray of light. I wanted a companion who was open about his emotions on any subject. I wanted a mate who would tell me the truth at the right time, even if it might hurt my feelings. He wasn't a big talker, but he always knew how to express himself with unparalleled acts of love. I wanted a man who would be loyal to me, someone who would stick by me when my beliefs were on the line. I wanted a person who was the epitome of kindness; a person who would go well out of his way to see a sick friend, help a person in need, and comfort a friend or a relative in their hour of tribulation. He was all that and more. Somehow, I managed to still be the same person. I didn't evolve by his presence. I was still shy with low self-esteem, insecurity, and a troubled mind filled with doubt. I was still carrying my negativity with him by my side. How could that be? I should have been reborn into something greater, like a flower that blossoms in the summer, yet the darkness that resided in me was still alive even though I was showered with an abundance of love. I decided to break free of that shell, and I decided to bet everything on our love. To mark the beginning of my new-found desire, I decided to celebrate us. I wanted to let him know that I would change so he could have the best version of me, and he was the sole reason that I wasn't afraid to take a step forward.

I wanted to create a dream night, and luckily for me, I had the imagination and the will to make it happen. The way I envisioned our date was beautiful. I was thinking about having a low-light type of night. I would use red and white mercury glass for the candles, with the sweet smell of roses. The sheets on the table would be red and white, and I would use the finest utensils we had. It would be the first time I spent so much time in the kitchen. On the menu, I planned to have roasted shrimp and peppers with creamy rice, and for dessert, a strawberry tart in the shape of a heart with a Valentine's smoothie, a combination of mango, apple, and grapes. I added coconut oil, almonds, and yogurt to this. For a healthy smoothie, I would also put raw cacao powder, and to get a little extra flavor, I would put cinnamon and vanilla extract. I hoped he would like it.

On top of that, I would also put red roses all over the stairs leading to my room. I would decorate my room with red, blue, pink, and white hearts that I would stick everywhere with gold and silver glitter on them. I would put red and pink petals inside the room... I think I was going a bit overboard with all this, but I wanted to show him how much he means to me. I had a brilliant idea to start the preliminaries in the bathroom with a warm bath. Inside it, I would put white roses. I couldn't wait for him to see me in my white pleated midi dress. My plan had no flaws. It was a guarantee that it would be a memorable night.

All that preparation for someone who existed on his own terms, who came and went as he pleased. I should have seen the pattern, but he always showered me with unconditional love that I could never see past the crumbs he threw my way.

The big day finally came; everything was set. I only had to wait for my lover to cross the door. After an hour, he didn't show up. I just noticed that I didn't have his number. He was always in front of my porch when I arrived from school. Why didn't I ask him for his number? Anyhow, he told me he would be present; he had to. Another hour passed. I went to check outside. I took a little walk. I could see from afar a storm heading my way. The wind was blowing. I went back home. Once inside, the phone rang. I rushed to it and picked it up. I answered the phone, all excited, but I was startled when I heard the voice of a stranger: "Hello, is this Lizzy?"

And just like that, my perfect night became a nightmare.

My POV

I responded, unsure of who was on the other side of the line: "Yes, why?"

"Sorry for calling you this late..."

I was nervous. I interrupted him in his dialogue and asked: "Who are you?"

I heard a heavy sigh, the kind that you do before telling someone something that might hurt them.

"Like I was about to say, I'm Inspector Adrien Johnson. I would like you to come to the station."

Once more, I interrupted him, stressed to let him proceed: "What for?"

The sergeant calmly responded:

"We have a John Doe here, and I believe that you will be able to identify this person, the only person."

The words hit me like a physical blow. Deep down, I already knew.

There was a heavy silence after this request. The sergeant proceeded to tell me, "I will send a patrol to pick you up."

"No, you can't."

I quickly hung up. There was only one possible scenario, and I didn't want to face it. The phone rang again and again and again. I decided to pick up. The sergeant followed with: "Lizzy, if I had other options, I wouldn't call you."

I stood there quietly; I needed to see it with my own eyes. I stopped the silent treatment and agreed to his demand.

Because sometimes you need to see the end of something beautiful to truly understand how thoroughly you've been destroyed.

I arrived at the station. Going up the stairs, I gazed upon the sky. The black clouds sprawled across the sky; the scent of rain was dark and heady. The eerie clouds were approaching us. Inside the hall, I was greeted by the sergeant. We walked toward the morgue without exchanging a word. We arrived in the cold basement. Lying on the table was a body covered with a sheet. We arrived in front of the body.

"Are you ready?" Adrien asked.

I simply nodded to tell him I was ready. When he removed the sheet, I was trembling in fear. My eyes started to twitch in panic as I lay eyes on the body. I couldn't believe it; it couldn't be him. I just couldn't accept that. Life had a way of toying with you. There was no guarantee; everything could be taken away from you in the blink of an eye. My lover was dead. I looked at his ghostly pale face; his lips were bluish. He looked so serene. Standing motionless, the detective understood that I knew him and gave me the room without saying a word. Alone with the cold body of my lover, I gently caressed his still face. I held his hand, wishing for the impossible. I managed to gather, in this circumstance, enough strength not to crumble. I took one last look at him, then gave him a long farewell kiss on the lips before exiting the room. Adrien was waiting for me on the other side. Seeing how devastated I was, he said, "I'm sorry."

Then Inspector Adrien received a call. While answering, he kept his eyes on me. When he hung up, he told me, "I won't be able to take your statement tonight. I'll ask an officer to bring you back home."

He proceeded to ask me, "We saw in our files that your grandmother is your legal guardian, but we couldn't reach her."

"I want to go home now."

"Sorry. I won't hold you any longer. If you need to speak, give me a call. I could refer you to someone in our department."

He handed me his card. I took it without saying another word. I was then escorted by an officer back home. Before I knew it, I was already on my porch. I opened the door. As I stepped inside, the emptiness that was brewing in my heart was heavier, a sheer nothingness that somehow takes over and holds onto my soul.

My POV

Grief gave me the feeling that the weight of the world was collapsing on my shoulders, and there was nothing I could do to get out from under it except ending my adventure. That grief formed a hole in my heart equal to a thousand times what I could handle.

This is where I learned that losing someone you think you love can hollow you out completely.

My steps were heavy and my body weak. I went to the kitchen and contemplated the untouched feast I had prepared. I wanted to cry my heart out and destroy everything around me, but none of that was put into action. I looked at the setup, and I just left. I needed to wash away my pain. I walked up the stairs; every step made my head pound and my stomach curl from the inside. I closed the door of the bathroom. I looked at my own reflection, refusing to grasp the reality of the situation. I could hear stillness fall outside, and in the silence, came a low crackle of thunder, rolling to the pattering of tiny raindrops. Still facing myself, I couldn't understand why I wasn't crumbling on the floor, crying my soul out. Life was unfair to me. Why did I always have to suffer? Why was the universe against me? It kept robbing me of my loved ones. My brain was about to explode; I needed to stop questioning myself, just stop. Trying to quiet the noise, a wave of self-loathing came, choking me, making me scream out of my lungs, making me throw a punch with intense repugnance at the mirror, shattering it into pieces. My hand was shaking and filled with blood. I opened the cabinet and swallowed all the pain medicine that was available. I went inside the bath and let the water fill the tub. I was surrounded by the white petals; the water was warm.

A streak of hot silver split the sky. Staring into the emptiness, tears started to fall. I was alone with the echo of my agony. I kept losing and losing again, no matter what I did or didn't do. Why try to move forward? Why get up when we fall? Why fight when it's easier to give up? Tomorrow wouldn't be brighter; I wanted to purge all my sorrow in the vast ocean, but it wouldn't matter. I tried to embrace life, but in the end, I was always left alone. As I spiraled in this pool of despair, I only wanted to end my pain for good, so I did the unthinkable and opened my wrist with a piece of the broken glass.

This was my first real attempt to escape, not from life, but from the endless cycle of love and loss that seemed to define my existence.

My life was dripping away. I was waiting for the Grim Reaper. Everyone that I loved had been ripped away from me. This cruel world didn't want me to stand and make a name for myself; its only goal was to bury me. No worries, you won, bastard. The blood was turning my white petals red; I saw the simplest color tarnished by my blood. They would never be able to gain back their original color; the damage was done. In my last moments, I had nothing positive to reflect on, besides that I would have peace of mind and, above all, if I'm destined for it, be next to my lover. Exhausted, I slowly closed my eyes as my heartbeat slowly faded away. The weather was getting chaotic; the downpour went all in. As I pushed my last breath, Mother Nature roared the loudest thunder that resonated across the earth. Then, complete darkness.

Chapter 7

What was going on? I was floating mid-air; everything around me was silent. I couldn't even hear my heartbeat. In the middle of that void, I kept drifting motionless when suddenly I saw a light glow from afar. It was so bright, yet it didn't blind me. I felt something pulling me toward it. Within arm's length, I got pulled inside the light. I slowly opened my eyes; I was inside my bath, and the light was off. Looking through the window, the storm was still raging. Did I fall asleep? I got out of the bath and took my towel. I went to close the window, but when I turned, my step was halted when the thunder brightened the room to reveal a shadow standing in front of me. I was frightened when, in that moment of illumination, I saw reddish eyes scrutinize me. I couldn't move; the ominous presence that the shadow was exerting made me shiver. Suddenly, it took a step forward inside the room. I screamed in panic, "Stop!!! Don't come any closer!"

I grabbed the first thing that was within my reach to defend myself. The silhouette halted its step promptly. I was trapped. I stood there trying to plan my next move. My only option was the window. I took a deep breath; I slowly turned my ankle. Then the silhouette standing in front of me said in a nonchalant voice, "Don't be silly."

My heart was pounding even faster. He had read my intention. I froze; he took another step towards me. I shouted, "Who the fuck are you?!"

He stopped once more. He then told me in a reassuring voice, "I apologize. I didn't mean to scare you."

"Answer the question!!" I demanded.

"My name is Nathaniel, but you can call me Nathan."

"What are you doing here?!!" I asked frantically.

He laughed.

"What's funny?!!" I snapped.

"You didn't change."

"What?!!??!!??"

"I'm here because I answered the call."

"The call? What call!!? From whom!!?" I demanded.

Even in my confusion, some part of me was already responding to him. The way he looked at me, like I was something to be consumed.

Then the power came back, and what I saw standing in front of me was out of this world. Gasping for a second breath, the atmosphere changed drastically. A fresh current blew inside the room. The first thing that struck me was his eyes; they had a unique color of amber. I was charmed by that unique set of eyes; they had this radiance that gave me the irresistible impulse to be close to him. His long brown hair looked so soft. His skin was tanned. He had prominent cheekbones and a well-defined chin and nose. He was muscular, with muscles that rippled across every part of his body. He was a seasoned warrior. I had never seen a man with those astonishing features.

I stood there confused; my emotions shifted drastically. I shouldn't feel this relaxed in that situation. I asked him, "What do you want from me?"

"Nothing that you wouldn't offer me."

"Why don't you answer me properly?"

Then, without answering the question, he closed the distance between us. I didn't react to his approach. The tension in the air was intense; I felt my body burn up. Even though he was intimidating me, I felt no threat. With a graceful voice, he told me, "You. I want you."

I was enchanted by those fiery eyes. How could they express so much desire towards me? I felt like he wanted every part of me; the amount of lust that emanated from him made me horny. Examining him from head to toe, I turned red when I saw his cock.

He was well equipped; I couldn't close my mouth in front of that piece of meat. He took my hand. I asked him, "What are you doing?"

He placed my hand on his heart; the rhythm was glorious and appealing. I couldn't comprehend what was going on. I started caressing his muscular chest. I couldn't stop stroking my hand on his body. Before I knew it, we were holding hands together. They were warm, tender, and welcoming. Caressing my hand with his thumb in a soft circular motion, he kept his eyes on me. I was completely hypnotized by the aura that was wrapping me; my heart melted under the sight of those amber eyes. I was blinded by the unknown; my desire and my curiosity had the best of me as I slowly caressed his hand with my thumb in response, in circular motion while gazing into those unique set of eyes. I was under his spell; he was eating me alive with envy and an unparalleled lust enough to shatter every doubt I had. I was seduced by what was offered to me; my desire submitted to his will. He approached his head, letting his lips brush against mine in a hot, enthusiastic, and demanding way.

I put my hand behind his head and leaned it towards me, then we kissed. His lips were soft; the taste of them made me float. From there, we didn't stop this entwined connection. We kissed repeatedly; each one was more passionate than the last one. Holding my chin up, we went at it for a moment. Then he slowed the tempo down and whispered slowly my name, prolonging each letter as if to savor them. My heart fluttered at his voice as I clasped my hands on either side of his face, and we went back to an ungovernable barrage of kisses. As we took another breather, he removed my soaking towel and took a long look at me with lust. My body hungered for him to quench the fire that was burning inside me.

We went on, embracing each other. I could feel his cock rubbing on me, poking me as blood relentlessly pumped it ferociously. I brought my hand down to grab his shaft and squeeze it as hard as I could. His dick was so stiff I couldn't help it; I started to energetically jerk his cock while pressing it like a sponge, while our tongues danced abundantly together. He firmly grabbed my ass, hard enough to leave a mark on it, then lifted me up to bring me inside my room. Once in there, he kept kissing me vigorously before bringing me to my knees. Facing his genitals, he held my chin up and looked down at me with a smile. He slowly rubbed his thumb around my lips, gently put it in my mouth, and moved it around. I seductively started to suck it; seeing the veins all pumped on his cock made my nipples hard. I took his dick inside my hand and slowly jerked him. I panted, then leaned forward and kissed the tip of his erect dick; it was weird, but I liked it, so I kept going. Then I began running my tongue around the head of his cock. I could feel the veins on his genitals pumping in my hand. Aroused, I didn't want to stop there. I opened my mouth and started slurping on his cock assertively. He grasped a handful of my hair and brought his dick deeper in my mouth; saliva was dropping like a waterfall as I gagged on his shaft. His wet cock in my mouth, he moaned as I coughed on his hard dick. Pulling my head out for a breather, he quickly brought me back to work. This time he was thrusting inside my throat back and forward so fast it made me tear up. Hands on his thighs, he went on a full ride with my throat. Then came all his sweet juice inside my filthy mouth.

Even in the intensity of it, I felt like an object being used rather than a person being loved. But I mistook his hunger for devotion.

I pulled my head, letting his cock out of my mouth, followed by a huge stream of cum that drooled out of my mouth. His hard cock kept squirting, so I furiously grabbed his dick and stroked him. Seeing his legs shake made me jerk him faster, making him cum again, but this time it splattered all over my face. I spread his cum all over my body. I slowly slid my sticky hand inside my vagina. What a weird sensation. I swallowed the rest of the cum, and to my great surprise, it didn't taste like I expected. I couldn't believe that after these two bursts of his load, his dick was still in frenzy. I was wet, I was sweating, I was sticky, and above all, amorous. I climbed on the bed, lying on my chest with my ass up and my wet vagina exposed to him. He got on his knees behind me and groped my ass, spreading them, and started eating my asshole like it was an open buffet. Then, without warning, he slipped his dick into my vagina in one big thrust, causing me to groan deeply in pain. I couldn't react as he held my hips and fiercely began thrusting into me. He was destroying my pussy; holding on to the sheets, I could feel the cum gushing inside my tight, wet pussy.

He didn't hold back; he went for a series of hard smacks on my ass. I didn't want to ruin the moment, so I brought my face to the nearest pillow and bit on it as hard as I could while he kept fucking me with deep, hard, steady strokes. He finally slowed down, only to spit on my asshole before fingering my butt. I wasn't expecting that; the way he maneuvered hurt me. I shouted in pain when he decided to force his large cock inside my ass. With no strength in my knees, I lay flat on the bed. He kept pounding me, then lifted me with his arm under my belly and suddenly grabbed a handful of my hair, pulling it to force me into a doggy-style position. He groaned repeatedly as his hips clapped against my ass. I felt his dick swell and throb, then he pulled out quickly to put me on my back, and without laying an eye on me, he held my two legs up with a tight grip, almost folding me in two, and went inside my vagina in full thrust without any warning. He kept rocking me like an animal, pounding me with brutal thrusts back and forward, destroying my delicate pussy. I became merely a participant; it felt like he was only fulfilling his needs at my expense at this point. He pushed one last moan before exploding his thick cum inside my vagina, making his load rush inside my womb. There was so much cum that a handful was dripping out of my pussy. Laying on the bed, sweaty and all wet, I felt like a whore. How could I let myself get roughly penetrated to the point it brought me tears of pain? Was that the right way of doing it? Was I a tool? At this point, it didn't matter; I was pleased by this raw, naughty spark. I was exhausted; I couldn't make anything out of it. Unable to stay awake, I gradually closed my eyes into total darkness. Suddenly, I woke up frantically. As I looked around, my head started spinning.

This was the first time I confused violence with passion, pain with pleasure. The first time I thought being used meant being wanted.

I took a breather. Then I got off the bed and went around the house to find Nathan. I kept searching by calling him out. I inspected every room, but no one was there. He managed to secure my soul in the palm of his hand. I had an uncontrollable urge for him to be by my side; otherwise, I feared I'd go insane. I started to feel weak; my body ached, and I struggled to think rationally. Still sore from our encounter, I was still craving him. He was all I needed, all I wanted. He was my world. I'd do anything for him: lie, steal, kill, just to be by his side. He would be my eternal flame, and I, his eternal slave. Wake up, Lizzy!!!! It only took one encounter for me to fall madly in love with him. If people knew what was going on, they would call me crazy and forlorn. He did something to me; I couldn't help myself. I was craving that never-ending energy. I became addicted to his whole person. As I screamed his name in desperation, what I thought would be a whimsical and perfect adventure became a nightmare. The human body is capable of sex long before the mind is mature enough to handle the emotions that go with it. Sex isn't just a fun thing like laser tag or bungee jumping; it is a powerful union between two souls. Isn't that why we say "lovers"? Sex should always be an act between two souls who love one another deeply, who are committed to one another, for it is a deeply spiritual act that bonds. As a species, we are happiest with lifelong mates. That is why older adults often caution young people not to run too fast, to take time and be sure. To feel the heady passion that sex brings without the love to keep the bond strong ultimately brings damage that is not easily repaired. That is why we need to utterly understand the difference between passionate love and lust. One builds strong relationships, keeps our souls healthy and our self-esteem high; the other is fireworks in the moment but ultimately leaves us empty, shallow, and, for some, addicted. What we had wasn't love, and yet I was obsessed with Nathan; he was the only thing on my mind. I didn't care if the world was burning; I wanted him back by my side. Wasn't I good enough? Maybe I scared him;

maybe he saw me as a waste of time. I thought I couldn't lose more, but the way he left me stranded affected me.

I mistook intensity for intimacy, confused being consumed with being cherished. I gradually became emotionally unstable, bursting into blind rage against anyone who dared to look at me the wrong way. I became a nightmare; I wished I could have just sat down with someone and talked about what bothered me, but it was way too late for me to reach out for a helping hand. I was struck by a mixture of emotions that were constantly unpleasant.

If someone had the nerve to talk to me about my recent debacle, I would recoil faster than a snapped high-tension spring to erase them. They were all hypocrites pretending to care for my well-being. I wasn't the shy, needy, lonely geek anymore; I was a wolf. In the middle of their judging eyes, I did feel caught and trapped, but that only grew my resentment for them. I was fueled by an intense rage; everyone and everything became my enemies. Every time I blew up, I was saying to myself that it wasn't my fault. Those who received my wrath were just in the wrong place at the wrong time. There was the explosion, and then the mental framework afterward to avoid guilt, to avoid owning the shame that was mine. That's how I stayed so foolish, so immature, refusing to open my eyes, sacrificing who I was to nourish a pristine ego that wasn't mine to begin with.

Then, one day, Nathan just reappeared in front of me. I couldn't believe my eyes; it felt like I hadn't seen him for years. Nothing was the same from the moment we met. He had been on my mind like a cancer. When I laid my eyes on him, my mind was made; I wouldn't let him go out of my sight anymore. His beauty, his soul, his flaming eyes that were a painting for my sight alone would be mine alone. Catching a whiff of his sweet and subtle scent, it drowned me in a fantasy world. I would be his only lover; I would be the only thing he would desire and think about. I would bear all his children. He would be mine by any means necessary. I couldn't care less why he left me without a word; I was just glad he was within my reach again.

"I was looking for you," I said breathlessly.

"I'm here," he replied simply.

I hugged him.

"I will always be a part of you," he whispered.

"You promise?" I asked desperately.

He calmly whispered to me, "I promise."

"I believe you," I breathed.

I couldn't believe those words came with ease out of my mouth. Once those words pass through your mouth in the light of day, they travel into your immediate surroundings like invisible bullets. These bullets split to enter the ears of others nearby, and they travel back inside your brain. In a split second, they have become much bigger words than you could have imagined. Those words could heal and build up, or they could wound and tear down. I was so excited that I could have brought the brightest light into the abyss. Ecstatic, I invited him over to my place for a lovely dinner, which he accepted. I looked at him, and there was a softness in his eyes. His eyes glistened in the light. I looked down, afraid that if I stared any longer, I would ruin our moment. With one finger under my chin, he lifted my head. He touched his forehead to mine, and I felt a warmth that filled my body from head to toe, invigorating me and filling me with passion and hope. He leaned his head closer to me, and his lips met mine. Gentle but passionate, he pressed his lips into mine. The world around me was erased; my heart fluttered, cherishing the luck to experience this moment once more. He put one hand on the back of my head and the other one near my lower back, pulling me closer to him. We pulled back; with a huge smile on my face, I said, "See you tonight."

For the occasion, I decided to prepare the perfect night for us, with the money I had stolen from Grandma. My plan was meticulously organized; I would begin with a delightful dinner. I planned to make the boyfriend steak, the sexiest piece of meat I had ever made. Let's not forget about the dessert; I would make a double chocolate profiterole. It was pastry puffs filled with chocolate ice cream and drizzled with dark chocolate sauce to make an elegant finale to a romantic meal. I would set the table in the kitchen with a nice, rich tone of purple and blue antique hydrangea alongside the softer pinks of winter roses. In this unusual combination, I would mix in some dark-centered anemone with the soft green tones of eucalyptus. I draped my table with an indigo-colored, pin-tuck satin tablecloth and placed a flower arrangement down the center of the table inside a beautiful vase. I would use mercury glass containers for my candles to add that eclectic, romantic look I wanted. With preparation all done, I was just waiting for the man who never left my mind.

Looking through the window, I saw black clouds sprawl across the sky; I shivered with an uneasy feeling. The door unlocked; Nathan walked in. We sat down at the table, ready to eat. I barely ate. I was too busy gazing at him enjoying his food. We didn't share a word; cutting through his perfectly cooked steak, I understood how pleased he was. As he took his last bite, I dabbed his fleshy cheeks with a delicate napkin. I went to sit back in my chair. He thanked me for the meal and told me he had to leave.

He didn't answer. I waited for him; he was mine, he had to stay, so I bluntly said, "You can't leave; I'm pregnant."

The lie came so easily. I was already learning to use whatever weapon I had to keep someone from abandoning me.

A sinister silence was filling the air. The scent of rain was dark and heady, as I gasped at the disappointment in his facial expression. He put the utensil down; head down, he let a sigh out, moving his head left and right in disapproval. He chuckled, then lifted his head while looking at me; the fire in his eyes had been doused with ice, making his amber eyes darker. I didn't want to lose him; I couldn't live without him, and if my body wasn't enough to keep him, maybe the knowledge of an unborn child would keep him by my side. I was obsessed with him so much that I became dependent on whatever he was offering me. If I had to be the manifestation of evil to be with him, I would do it without any doubt. I would take every path to chain him to my soul. Trying to press the matter, I nervously told him, "Don't worry; we will do great together."

Then he got up and calmly advanced towards me; his energy shifted to someone completely different, and with an angry tone, he said, "If you love someone, you'll sacrifice yourself; you'll walk right into the flames and never blink or look back. If you love someone, you'll give them the things they need at the expense of yourself."

The atmosphere became breathless. My plan was deviating from its intended course, and I sensed a sinister and malevolent presence affecting me. Every step he took created an alarming sensation of a fight or flight situation. Stillness fell over the street, and in the silence came a low crackle of thunder, rolling across rooftops to the pattering of tiny raindrops. I quickly grabbed a knife and screamed out of fear, "Stop!!! Don't come any further!"

This was the moment I learned that love and violence could exist in the same breath, that someone could desire you and destroy you simultaneously.

He ignored my command and kept coming at me.

"You know you can't lose what you never had," he said coldly.

Then, without a care in the world, he slapped me with the back of his hand. The hit was so vicious that it brought me to the floor; blood was dripping from my mouth. Still coming at me, he pushed the chair out of his way. I quickly began to crawl towards the knife that had fallen out of my hand. Before I could reach it, he grabbed me by the hair and pulled me up, bringing me to my feet. As he looked at me in the eyes with an empty void, I begged him to stop. He went for a series of hard punches to my stomach. He lifted me up and threw me on the table, destroying everything. Food and utensils were spread all over the place; drinking glasses and plates were shattered. A few pieces pierced my skin, but the way the table fell made an obstacle between us. Believing I had sufficient time to reach the nearest exit, I attempted to flee, but Nathan's swift response thwarted my efforts. I grabbed a chair and held it tight to create an obstacle between me and Nathan. In a position of dominance, he toyed with me by taunting me about the direction he would take to attack, smirking like the devil himself. We both knew he could easily remove the chair, so I decided to hit him with the chair. He effortlessly grabbed the chair mid-air, ripped it from my hand, and gave me a good swing with it. He didn't hold back, sending me flying out of the kitchen. I was still on my feet; rushing towards me, I took a frame off the wall and swung it at his face. I made a big cut on his nose. He responded by giving me a right hook. I was still on my feet; he grabbed me and slammed me into the wall. He stood in front of me and gave me a series of combinations with his fists. Confident he had the upper hand, he let down his guard. I took all the strength I had to kick him in the groin. He crumbled down to his knees. I went to the kitchen, took a chair, and swung it across his head. Out of breath, I took a minute to catch my breath. I went for the phone to call for help, but he was already back on his feet. I took a few steps back.

"You bitch!! Who do you think you are!!" he roared.

Then he rushed towards me; I quickly grabbed the knife lying on the ground and stabbed him in the shoulder as he tackled me against the edge of the counter. He got up and was laughing while removing the knife. I crawled away from him. He turned me onto my back and choked me with his foot, then he stopped when I was about to pass out. He stomped on my stomach once. Unable to move, he did it again and again and again. Thinking he was done with me, he proceeded to launch a series of hard kicks all over my body until he was exhausted. I was nothing more than a pebble on the road.

"Thanks for the ride," he said with a cruel smile.

And with those words, I learned that I could be used up and discarded like garbage. That my value was only what I could provide to someone else.

Coughing blood, I watched him walk away before passing out. He had violated every inch of my body. When I regained consciousness, I looked at my surroundings; my vision was blurry, and I saw black and white dots popping in front of my eyes. Breathing was a challenge, but with the help of the railing, I managed to get up the stairs. The pain throbbed in my guts; it was deep, like someone had their hand in there, squeezing my organs. I couldn't even stand straight.

Wincing in pain all the way to the bathroom, I carefully removed my clothes. I took out pieces of glass that had penetrated my skin. I looked at some of my injuries; my abdomen was purple and lumpy where it should be smooth. My back was beaten; my head was a bloody mess. I could barely stand on my two feet. I went inside the warm bath I made; the water was caressing my body, but I couldn't remove any of my pain. Physically and mentally, I was completely obliterated. A streak of hot silver split the sky. The rain was falling, splashing heavily on everything it could touch. Alone in a fetal position in the bath, the water was turning red. How could I be so childish? How could I be so desperate? How could I be so stupid? Me, smart? What a shitload of misplaced ego. I was just a frail brat searching for...

Connection. Love. Someone to tell me I mattered. But I kept finding people who taught me the opposite.

My body was numb; swallowing all of my grandmother's pills was the only lucid thing I did. With the extent of my injuries, I needed medical aid, but why bother? Waking up another day in this world wasn't worth it. My body was cold; my skin was pale; my lips turned blue. No matter the path I took, it seemed happiness wasn't in the cards for me. I always ended up making the wrong decision or acting the wrong way. I was born with shackles; regardless of my plans for tomorrow, I was doomed to fail. I wasn't a 'good product' for this world. I had lost myself along with everyone that was dear to me.

Some wounds never heal. They just teach you to expect less from the world and from yourself.

The wind was blowing inside the room; I had reached my limit. My shoulders sank below the level of the water. I couldn't even move a muscle; I welcomed death not with a smile or fear, but like

My POV

a valet holding the door open for me. The downpour was fading away, and as I pushed my last breath, a ravaging thunder blasted so hard that it could awaken the dead. Then, total darkness.

Chapter 8

I was relaxed; the water felt good on my skin. With my head on the edge of the bath, I took a deep breath before opening my eyes. I could hear the smooth rain falling. The percussion of the falling water varied according to the surface it wetted. It was a real symphony to my ears; the atmosphere was perfect. Everything was so calm when a sweet breeze blew the scent of this aphrodisiac perfume that filled my nose once more. The odor simultaneously induced euphoria and relaxation in my mind and body. The smell felt like I was guided from harm's way, like a safe passage out from a nightmare.

"Hmmm," I murmured.

What was this smell?

"Hmmm," I sighed again.

Rejuvenated, I stretched myself when I felt I poked something. It was cushy and soft. It felt like I was rubbing my feet on someone's skin. I lifted my head to see if my intrusive thoughts were trying to deceive me. Then, when I laid eyes on what was in front of me, I had no words to express what was going through my mind. I completely froze. In front of me, there was someone inside my bath. I couldn't move; my soul went knocking at the door of heaven.

"Hello, sunshine," the stranger said warmly.

In disbelief, I couldn't comprehend how a stranger kneeling inside my bath could give me an absolutely trustworthy vibe. I bluntly asked, "Why are you here?"

"For you, love," she replied gently.

A tear fell as I smiled; for some reason, I felt she understood my pain better than anyone else. The way she said it felt like a mother tending to her worried pup. The sound waves she was producing with her mouth made my body vibrate with every syllable. When her eyes locked onto mine, they weren't shy and insecure like mine. They were confident, dominant, and sincere. She had the kindest pair of hazel eyes, which let you see in and out of her very being. They were a deep pool of restless gold, an ocean of hope and possibility. As I gazed into her eyes, I could feel her. Her eyes radiated extraordinary brightness, embodying life itself. She was making her own path; nothing could break her or let the world break her. I trembled in admiration. Then, with a flirting voice, she told me, "Hi, cutie."

I turned red; her voice was charming. I blushed and laughed nervously; I couldn't keep my eyes off her. Her face was as pure as the first raindrop from heaven. Her hazel eyes illuminated the room. She had a radiant face with a brilliant shine, a small nose, and the curves on her luscious lips had an answer for everything. Her dark hair, cascading down, looked so soft. She giggled, seeing how much in awe I was. She kept her divine eyes on me. I was attracted to her in ways that surprised me; she was melting me with her carnal smirk. Without any hesitation, she bluntly told me in a seductive tone, "Kiss me."

I was caught off guard. Stuttering while answering, I said, "Wh...wh...wh...at? Ex...ex...ex...cuse me.... what?!?..."

I couldn't believe the audacity she was displaying. She kept eating me alive with her eyes, then said, "Don't be shy. They are yours."

I was baffled; she licked her lips in a sensual way, exercising intense arousal pressure. I was flabbergasted by her proposal. Even though I wanted her lips on mine, why would someone like her waste her time receiving a kiss from a simpleton? I couldn't say a word; I kept my mouth open, absorbed by the dilemma that was presented to me. Then she closed my mouth and leaned her head toward me.

"I decided for you," she whispered.

My heart was racing a thousand miles per hour; she was coming for a kiss. She tenderly put her hand behind my head and gradually brought it to her without applying any force. I let her lead the dance. The moment our lips touched, the world vanished instantly. That kiss was so heavenly tender, expressing a burst of unmatched love. It was a connection that showed me the strength of her feelings for my miserable self. What she was giving me wasn't for mere pleasure; she was giving me something far greater than that. It was literally a soul-matching moment. Leaning on me as our breasts were rubbing against each other, she kept kissing me; my brain was about to explode. I succumbed to that fervent kiss; a warm sensation spread through my entire body. She firmly grabbed my hair and kissed me with more intensity; her tongue deep inside my mouth, she pulled out a string of saliva that was hanging between our lips. I wanted to slurp it inside my mouth. My mind was racing with dirty, nasty, kinky thoughts. What I wanted to do to her was far from who I was. I was overcome by a nymphomaniac's behavior. She wiped away the string of saliva with her thumb while maintaining eye contact with me, exhibiting complete composure. She knew how to approach me, understanding well that I was complex and not easily decipherable. This increased my interest in her.

The way she presented herself felt like an invitation. Like I was being asked to discover something beautiful about myself.

I slowly licked my lips without leaving her out of my sight; looking at her brought me such voracity that my desire went out of control. The excitement I showed on the outside couldn't adequately reflect what I felt inside. Every neuron in my brain was hypercharged. All the muscles in my body were stiff, trying to contain my urge not to go all over her like a wild beast. The way she smiled and looked at me was making me go crazy. How could she have so much aura? Only fondness was floating in the room. She held me down with one hand and positioned her crotch on top of one of my legs, and while looking at me with this delightful smirk, she began to grind against my leg. She started to kiss down my neck while playing with my hard nipples. Then, before I knew it, her tongue was inside my mouth. We tangled with devotion.

Letting her genitals rub against my leg, I wiggled it a bit so she could enjoy it even more. Suddenly, I felt her fingers slide along my thigh all the way between my legs. I could only stare at her, eager for the next step. She gently rubbed my vulva, making me moan at her simple yet delicate touch. Then she brought our interaction to another level as she thoroughly inserted her finger inside my pussy. She gradually started to thrust her finger with inhuman precision. I could feel my soul leaving my body; I was getting aroused beyond comprehension as my eyes rolled backward like I had been exorcised. She grabbed my hands and brought them to her voluptuous breasts. I was hers; I belonged to her and her only. She knew how to dominate without inflicting pain as she inserted more fingers inside my vagina.

My body went into spasms as I orgasmed uncontrollably; she was enjoying the way my body responded to her touch. She kept going, making me hold on for my dear life on the edge of the bath. She went faster than I ever thought was possible, making me squirt without restraint. She then stopped and removed her hand as I felt a discharge going through my body. Her hand was covered with my juices; she gave me an arousal smirk and licked her hand while keeping eye contact with me. I was mesmerized by her carefree attitude. Unable to close my mouth in awe, she put her hand inside my mouth.

"Taste it," she commanded softly.

I went on licking every finger. She licked her lips, got up, and stood in front of me.

"I want you," she said with certainty.

On my knees inside the bath with the water almost drained, I was in the presence of someone wondrous. She had that movie star look. Not overly tall and willowy, but more like an action star. Her muscle definition was perfect, and she glowed with unwavering confidence. She wasn't just flawless in her bone structure; her skin was like silk over glass, and she radiated intelligent beauty. Her breasts were firm and big; her curves were out of this world. The water was everywhere on the bathroom floor. Standing in front of me, she grabbed my wet hair and pulled my face to her crotch. With a commanding, yet also sensual voice, she said, "Eat me."

I didn't think twice as I dove with my mouth wide open, covering her pussy. I gently began to flick along the edges with my tongue. She started to thrust her hips against my mouth, forcing my tongue to go deep inside her. Her juices tasted marvelously and made me go crazy as I spread her legs and held them down as I ate her furiously. Her moans were out of this world as she held down my head, pressing her genitals against my mouth. I could literally drown in it without any regret as I enjoyed this unique meal. After relentless tongue play, she decided to let go of my head. Then she started caressing my face, and with determination in her eyes, she said, "Make me cum."

She made me feel that her entire being was mine and nothing could interrupt this. My pussy was dripping wet. I slowly inserted one finger. It was so smooth.

"Don't be shy," she encouraged.

She grabbed my wrist and pushed all my fingers into her vagina. I didn't hesitate and complied with her desire. Thrusting her in a good rhythm, she kept caressing my face with her delicate hand while she moaned. It was an unbelievable sensation. With her soft touch alone, she could fire me up.

"Faster," she breathed.

I was fisting her faster and harder. She pulled my hair backward while moaning with intense lust; I wanted her to cum all over me. I could feel her body tighten, but amazingly, she was still in control. Then she stopped my movement, looked at me with a satisfied look, and then she brought me out of the bath. She lay me on my back on the wet floor. In a position of dominance, she looked down on me with a smile that could melt hell. She told me, "I love you."

She brought her delightful pussy to my face and started to ride it. She took my hand and put it on her voluptuous breasts; unfortunately, my hand wasn't big enough to properly hold one of those beauties. I spread the edges of her vulva and started eating her out once more. She firmly grabbed her breasts while using her exquisite tongue to lick and generously suck her nipples. Then she pinched my nipples while thrusting her hips back and forward. Even though this part of our encounter was hurting me, she brought her face in front of my genitals and started to eat me out. I duplicated the pattern she was using with her tongue and fingers, but I couldn't follow for long as she made me cum again and again. We switched positions and started to guzzle each other passionately in a majestically perfectly placed sixty-nine. In the heat of the moment, I frantically sucked her clit. She let out a primal cry as she came all over my face. Her legs were shaking as she showered me with her hot squirt, squeezing my thigh with her hand with every spasm she got.

"You are feisty," she panted.

I couldn't stop there. I went back to fisting her. The way she moaned was powerful. She squirted; with my mouth wide open, I attempted to drink it all. Breathing heavily, she said, "Well... done."

After catching her breath and regaining her composure, she got up and extended her hand to help me get to my feet. She grabbed my towel, then looked straight at me like she knew everything that needed to be known about me. I wondered what she was thinking. Did she see all my flaws, my insecurities, my low self-esteem, my anxiety? I'm pretty sure she was mocking me inside her magnificent head. She must have realized how pathetic I was and used that to approach me with ease. She would eventually give up on me. Why would she stick around someone who doesn't have a backbone? But she was something out of this world. She handed me a towel, and with the smoothest voice, she said, "Don't worry. I'm all yours."

She walked out naked from the bathroom. She wasn't shy to show her curves, knowing she had everything to please. It was frightening yet so desirable. She stopped at the door frame, then slightly turned her head and said, "Oh, I almost forgot... My name is Angela."

She left me astounded; she was something else compared to me. She was the girl I had always dreamed of being. She was strong, sexy, and smart. With her, today was a given; tomorrows were only a concept. Everyone was her friend, and judgment wasn't her thing. She slid effortlessly between social groups, and she enjoyed competition in any form. She flowed through life like water; she was carefree, and it seemed nothing could hurt her. She was above everything. She was simply perfect. She loved me without any doubt; her devotion to seeing the best in me was fearless. No matter how many times I fell into the whirl of my flaws, she picked me up and polished me; she was the embodiment of a phoenix, one who had suffered, turned to ash, and been reborn as this tempting creature. She showered me with unconditional love. She gave me a long-awaited transformation; she gave me unshakable confidence. Her love for me only grew as I changed every aspect of who I was to become who I should be, who I wanted to be. In this rawness, in this absolute vulnerability, I harnessed her leadership to confront everything that was set in my way. My personality changed; my entire life changed. I was in the driver's scat. Without her, I wouldn't be able to do that. She gave me her energy, her time, and mostly her love. She helped me beat my demons. She chose me; she understood me; she was making me better in every aspect of my life. She allowed me to walk away from the well-trodden path that I had built for myself. She guided me to be creative and to know that complexity and intelligence weren't the same thing; simplicity was smart. I saw beyond the wall of despair. Without her, I would be stuck forever in my own negative mind, thinking of loneliness. She made me see and believe how special I was. No more shame, no more low self-esteem, no more darkness, no more solitude, no more emptiness, no more pain. She loved me regardless of who I was. She put me on the path I had always wanted to be on. She helped me become someone that I had always dreamed of being. I wasn't a weight that needed to be carried; I was alive; I was breathing life, and by walking this path, I saw the anger, the jealousy, the envy, and the hate of those who were below me. My greatness was a cancer; they wished to shine their light and flourish like me, but couldn't.

I was becoming a reflection of her, comfortable in the bed I'd made for myself.

I was in control; I dictated the flow of my life. My circle of friends grew. My past was just a sad dream. I was in the best condition of my life. In the storm of this amazing improvement and empowerment, I became popular; my ego grew so fast, but my happiness was too greedy to let me see that. I felt unstoppable; I was attracting only positivity. Every day, I felt like a queen. As my popularity began to rise, the situation intensified when I was approached by a teen magazine for a feature in their monthly illustration. At that moment, I understood that I had the opportunity to share my voice with the world. An opportunity of that nature was rare. I was given the chance to connect with individuals who felt trapped like I did. I could become their guiding light. Everything was going beyond any of my wildest dreams. I reached a level in my life that felt like the sky had no limits. I craved the spotlight; I was brighter than the sun itself. I was courageous, fearless; I was a warrior, and my shining armor was made of diamond. I was rushing toward the path that was laid out before me without a second thought. But during my newfound self, Angela's attitude started to change drastically. She wasn't the same girl anymore; it felt like her thunder was locked tight in a cage.

In that period, she made it clear she didn't like who I was becoming, but she was jealous. I could feel it; I could see it. She wanted to stop me from reaching new heights. As a matter of fact, she tried to keep me on a tight leash, but I was reborn and easily broke free from her paws. I was my own person, and I didn't plan to go back to my old self; I wouldn't let anything tarnish my new light. I went from nothing to something. If I were in her place, I would also be blinded by my metamorphosis. I discreetly distanced myself from her. I didn't want her by my side; she had become an obstacle that I needed to pass to move forward. She wouldn't understand. I wasn't an outcast anymore; I wasn't the dirt under the boots. I was free from the jail society had built for me.

Our relationship was becoming mediocre, but before everything went up in flames, Angela proposed that we have a special date at my place to salvage what we used to have. I couldn't refuse her proposition; she was still the one who had made me break free from my shell. She had removed the moon from the sun and let the rays of hope, love, and strength shine upon me.

Knowing her, I should be expecting to be welcomed with a blue and white theme all over the place. There would be nice navy blue, sky blue, and white floating balloons, with a few of them tied together on my left and right. She would set the lighting with a little dim blue, giving you the impression of being inside the ocean. A set of tables that would leave me speechless. Instead of wrapping utensils in cloth napkins, she would display pretty linens by laying them flat and corralling flatware with a white ribbon underneath her blue sky napkins. The table would be covered by a white sheet with a pattern of blue flowers all over the place, and dinnerware that would match her theme. For dinner, I'm seeing a delicious sheet pan steak and veggies. It's simple, but Lord, it's delightful. Navy blue, sky blue, and white petals would be making their way straight to the bathroom with a nice bath waiting for us, with the sweet aroma of a saltwater bath bomb.

Ready to join her for a romantic evening, I got delayed by a local magazine that wanted an interview about my recent achievements. Everyone was showering me with praising words. It was gratifying to see people who would have looked down on my past self being so enraptured. Before going home, one of my friends wanted to celebrate. At first, I refused since I had plans with Angela, but she managed to convince me it wouldn't take long. After she told me where we were going, I realized it was a small detour, so I went along with her. When we arrived at our location, I was welcomed by a group of friends. They were all there for me. I let all the glorifications sink in and went on to enjoy the party to the fullest. I didn't see how fast time flew by; I needed to get back home. Hailing a cab, I could see black clouds sprawl across the sky. I didn't even warn Angela that I would be late. I had been such an asshole to her lately. I stood her up, but she would surely understand when I explained everything to her.

On my way home, I was drained. I just wanted to take a bath and go to bed. I arrived home. When I arrived at the kitchen, I smiled when I saw her preparation matched my predictions. She was sitting at the table with a disappointed look on her face.

"Where have you been?" Angela asked coldly.

"Ugh, honestly, I am really, really sorry," I replied quickly.

"You just don't care anymore," she said flatly.

"Listen, I can explain. I was with some friends..." I started to say.

She interrupted me and said with a wretched attitude, "Oh... I see."

I was baffled by the amount of hostility she was projecting toward me and went into defense mode, "Stop with that ridiculous attitude. I'm sorry, but I'm here now. So, like I was saying..."

She interrupted me once more and said with an insouciant tone, "Whatever, I don't want to know."

We sat down without exchanging a word. I looked at my plate. I wasn't hungry, but I couldn't add salt to her injury, so I took a few bites.

"If you don't like it, don't eat it," Angela said sharply.

"No! No! It's not that!" I protested.

"What's the problem? Not up to your new standards?" she asked with venom.

"Geez, what do you mean by that?" I snapped.

"Nothing," she replied dismissively.

This was the moment everything started to unravel.

I was angry; the tension was at its highest. I slapped the table with anger and said, "Damn! I already told you I'm sorry!!! I tried to explain, but you want to play stupid games!!"

She sat there without reacting to my outburst. She looked at me and said, before taking a pause, "You know what, Lizzy."

"What?!?" I demanded.

In a sad tone, as she went back to eating, she said, "Never mind."

I looked at her and didn't say anything. What a pitiful sight. I couldn't stomach that ugly look anymore. It irritated me, but I managed to calm my nerves. I closed my eyes and took a deep breath. As I breathed out, she asked me in a diffident voice, "Do you still love me?"

"Oh, come on, of course! Why ask that stupid question?" I replied defensively.

"Well, we don't interact like we used to. Since things are going your way, you push me aside."

"So, what do you want from me?" I asked defensively.

She looked at me straight in the eyes, and this time with a bit of frustration, said, "Stop acting like a bitch."

"A what now?!?" I exploded.

I felt disgusted by her attitude; my emotions were boiling up. I wanted to hurt her. Something that I never thought was possible to manifest against her. I was repulsed by what I was seeing; she had become weak, insecure, needy, possessive, and above all, jealous. Her new personality turned me upside down. I got up and walked out of the kitchen. I took one last look at her like royalty looking down on a peasant. I felt unstoppable; I felt the urge to roar like a wild beast. Guided by my newfound ego, I angrily told her in the most disrespectful manner, "You are pathetic. I can't stay near an unavailing person."

The words came out like poison. In that moment, I became everything I had once hated, everything that had ever hurt me.

My POV

I'll never forget her eyes. How the blast of flame coming out of my mouth burned her to ashes. I murdered her with those few words. The one person who loved me with all her soul. How could I be so ungrateful? I couldn't believe what I just said. How dare I? She was strong. That wouldn't affect her. As a matter of fact, it would boost her confidence, bring the light back to her eyes, and she would stop being so hopeless. So, instead of apologizing, I walked away with my pride, letting my words echo in a broken home.

The scent of rain was dark and heady. Sitting inside my bath, guilt was wrapping me. I had spat on her when she needed me the most; by doing so, I let her know she was loved only for her strengths, her dominance, her flamboyant traits, and unique personality. The way I pushed her aside as soon as she stopped showing me that.

I destroyed the person who loved me for who I was and not for who I became. I forgot what really mattered. With love, people could grow strong enough to whisper at the iron bars that held them to the point of bending them out of their way. Love could fix souls, fix brains, and cure pain, but time passed, and I wasn't giving her any of that. How could I step on her when she was at her lowest? How could I be proud of myself? I was only able to become who I was because she allowed me to embrace this venue. My new self got a good taste of this newfound life; I was ungrateful for her vulnerability. That deformed ego I cradled as my own self had allowed her to be the wind beneath my wings and not a bird soaring free. Meditating in this hot water, I started to wonder if I was the one who brought her to that miserable state. I neglected her when she had done nothing but love me. I must be the one who brought her to that miserable state. How didn't I see it? Why didn't I see it? I needed to fix this. I should apologize for that selfish behavior. I had gone too far. This wasn't who I wanted to become. It couldn't be.

Ready to get out of the bath, I felt her hand on my shoulder, holding me down.

"Ah!!! You scared me!" I gasped.

She didn't say anything. "Lis-

ten, I wanted..." I began.

Her grip started tightening on my shoulder.

"Ouch! Stop. That hurts!!!" I cried out.

"What the fuck are you doing, Angela?!?" I demanded.

The atmosphere was tense. In a broken voice, she said, "How dare you! You are the one who's worthless."

There was pain in her eyes... it was my pain.

Depression is the unseen, unheard, silent killer. It's the pain that's too much to cope with, too hard to deal with, and so misunderstood. You can't escape it, no matter how hard you try, because it follows you around like a black shadow that's on the inside. Loneliness eats you alive, swallowing every ounce of hope you had yet to spare. It feasts upon any happiness you have left, leaving behind an empty carcass, full of despair and memories you can't seem to hold onto anymore. It takes your heart into its claws, squeezing out every bit of life you had circulating throughout your opaque veins. I was afraid. I attempted to reason with her and her pain, but before I could utter another word, she pushed me under the water with those strong, soft, angelic hands. The adrenaline flooded my system like it was an intravenous drip right into my blood at full pelt. I tried to get out by spinning my body left and right, but she didn't budge. She was strong. Struggling to hold my breath, I thought my heart would explode; my eyes were wide open. During this distressful situation, I laid my eyes on her face. She was in pain; I knew this look. I was familiar with it, yet blinded by her presence.

The urgency for air was plainer than ever. I used my arms and legs to try to kick out, but the result was still the same. My arms were out of reach; she had full control over my body. By the second, the strength in my body went away. She was shouting, but I couldn't hear a word. I had let her down. "Love hurts," as they say, but it's a lie. Love heals; love makes people whole again, and love fills them with the goodness they need to be as kind and loving. What hurt was betrayal, thoughtlessness, uncaring attitudes, and careless gossip. What hurt was people being unfriendly, not welcoming a new person to a neighborhood, or making "exclusive" cliques that were defined by who was "not welcome." What hurt was bullying, harassment, selfishness, and greed, but love was also the greatest gift mankind ever received, a gift that lived on within us all. Love was a gift that needed nurturing. It was the truth within us that knew life could not be given a price tag. Love knew to be kind and never to hurt or kill. Love knew to treat anyone as yourself. Love was what we craved from birth, a craving that had to be met by our new and loving earth-bound family. Love knew that a life was worth more than a pair of new shoes or designer makeup. Love was what could save us, make us fully human again, and raise us up. Love was what I didn't give her, yet I didn't mind taking every bite of it from her.

Fighting for my dear life, I could see in her eyes the emptiness, the darkness that was flooding her. The light that made her who she was had been snuffed out. I was reaching the end of the line. How could I hate her? I had become a brat filled with envy, greed, and mostly pride. Oh, my dear Angela, how long had it been since you smiled? I had stolen everything from you. You gave me something precious, something unique, and yet I acted like I was the one who had made my own path to become my own light. I broke you for my own gain. I wished I could have acted before we came to this outcome, but know this... I don't hate you... I never hated you.

Stillness fell over the street, and in the silence came a low crackle of thunder, rolling across rooftops to the pattering of tiny raindrops. My head was pounding; my lungs felt as though they had been set on fire. I couldn't hold it any longer. I opened my mouth. The water went rushing inside my mouth. In a heartbeat, my lungs were full, gasping for air. I started to descend into a state of melancholy, behaving as though the world owed me happiness, which led to my becoming increasingly arrogant. I had used words sharper than a knife to wound someone who had removed a void inside me.

Desperately trying to push back, a series of flashes rushed through my mind. What I saw, what I felt, was so despicable, so ghastly, that my mind was in shambles, removing any desire to stay alive. In disbelief, I stopped fighting and let myself drown in the abyss. Accepting the outcome, in this watery coffin, I closed my eyes as the downpour began, accompanied by the loudest thunder that sent me off to the other realm.

But in that moment of surrender, something changed. A memory surfaced, clear and terrible.

"I re...mem...ber," I gasped.

Chapter 9

Now I remember the rest of it. The memory I've been running from.

The bell of the school rang, waking me up. What happened? Did I fall asleep? I looked at the time. School was over. I took my stuff and headed home.

Arriving at my bus stop, the rain started to fall rapidly, so I used the shortcut to the old bridge. Every step I was taking made the weather worse, so I decided to jog to my destination. While pursuing my path on this old road, an individual jumped out of the bushes nearby. I swiftly avoided him; from there, I didn't hesitate and went full throttle toward the bridge. I kept running with all my might, but the condition of the road wasn't ideal for the way I was running. The terrain was unstable, filled with mud, holes, and a variety of trash, but I kept going. Maintaining my speed ensured my safety. Familiar with the route, I skillfully evaded his attempt to seize me once more, causing him to slip on the wet grass. I kept moving forward. I made a hurdle over a barricade. When I landed, I lost my footing, making me lose some momentum.

Then, as I turned my head to see where he was, he pulled my hair and threw me on the ground. I rolled over and quickly got up. He then grabbed the front of my white ruffle blouse that was underneath my jean jacket and ripped it. In response, I gave him a hard kick in the nuts. Without wasting a second, as he stumbled, I turned around to flee, but I miscalculated his determination and the level of pain he could handle. On one knee, he grabbed me by the arm. Leaning toward me in pain, he kept an unrelenting hold on me. I couldn't break free from his hold by pulling, so I went with a series of strikes with everything I had to his face. Fists, slaps, even knees, but that only made his hold tighter. He regained his posture; angry, he raised his hand to slap me back and forth. Even though I was able to block it, the impact was hard.

After a few hits, he managed to hit me with a hard backhand. Having trouble maintaining my balance, the pain in my forearm was intense, extending through to the bone and causing my hands to tremble. Still on my feet, he let go of my arm and gave me a hard punch to my stomach that made me kneel. He pursued his attack with a kick with the sole of his shoe on my chest.

I was lying on my back; he went on top of me and completely ripped the front of my blouse wide open. I put my arms around his neck, held on tight and bit his nose with ferocity. I let my teeth claw into him like an alligator. I could taste his salty blood gushing into my mouth. He managed to get up; that was perfect for me since I was able to bring my legs around his waist for a better grip. He gave me a bear hug so tight I could feel my insides being reshaped. I could barely breathe, but there was no way I would let go.

He let go of me, then jumped toward the pavement. The concrete underneath the grass, plus his weight, gave me excruciating pain, yet I didn't loosen my grip. I could feel his flesh getting ripped apart. He got up and did it once more. I couldn't hold it, but I hurt him enough to have time to crawl away from him. With the help of the road barrier, I got up. He was kneeling in the mud, grabbing his nose, growling like a foul beast. I could feel every bone in my back cracking. What next? Could I outrun him? In my state, it was a gamble.

"YOU!! BITCH!! AAAAHHHHHH!" the aggressor screamed.

I picked up a stone and rushed toward him. I needed a permanent solution to eradicate this threat. I lifted the rock above my head, and when I reached a well-placed striking distance, I swung at his head, but he managed to avoid it partially. I stumbled but was still in control of my body. I was able to ground myself and swing one more time. This time, I was able to capitalize with a direct hit on the side of his head.

Both lying on this abandoned road, I observed the end of my path. I got up, almost out of breath; my back was killing me. The weather was heavy on my body. The rain was so cold; I wanted to curl up in front of a warm fire. On his knees, arms lying next to his body with his head down, he didn't move. His nose was holding on by a string, and the side of his head wasn't pretty.

I started walking toward the bridge. Then, a few meters from it, I got pulled by the hair and slammed to the ground. He dragged me away from the bridge; he struggled as I moved my body in all directions. He then stopped; he knelt on top of me and started punching. Every strike was with more intensity. I managed to protect my head, but he was relentless. He grabbed both of my wrists to move them apart. Then he bent his head and started licking my neck. He went next to my ear and said in a creepy, amused way as thunder struck in the sky, "You are mine."

As he salivated all over me, he bathed me with his blood. That bastard didn't have a nose anymore. I stopped resisting, thinking I had submitted to his will, he went to put his lips on mine, letting his guard down, so I bit his lower lip viciously, ready to rip it off his face. He grabbed my neck and applied pressure directly on my hyoid bone. I couldn't hold it. He spat a chunk of blood on my face, then he grabbed my head and slammed it on the concrete a couple of times. Unable to move, he kept giving me a barrage of punches.

The rain was washing away my blood. When he stopped, I was in bad shape; I couldn't open my left eye, I thought my jaw was broken, and my nose was bleeding profusely. I couldn't fight anymore.

He furiously ripped my blouse; my breasts were exposed in front of this pervert. He didn't waste any time and went for my nipples with his fetid, bloody mouth, sucking on them like a leech, squeezing my breasts like they were stress balls. Every part he touched made me lose my essence. He spread my legs, putting one of his knees on my right thigh. It was so heavy; the weight was crushing me. Then I felt something hard rubbing against my vulva. I gained a second breath, feeling the ground around me to find something useful. Stretching my arm, I finally managed to grab onto something; it was a sharp piece of rusty metal.

He ripped off my nice white pleated cheer skirt, revealing my floral panties. It was the only piece of clothing still intact on me. I waited for the perfect window. I was focusing on his jugular, holding the piece of metal so hard it made me bleed. He reached down to my panties and, with his filthy hand, started rubbing my vulva aggressively. He ripped my panties, pulling them so hard that the rest went inside my butt. His fingers clamped down on my nipples and squeezed them like he wanted to pour out milk from them. I felt his cock poking my vulva. Revolted, I was too hasty in my movement. I swung at him, but his posture allowed him to block my attempt, so I sliced his forearm.

The rusty metal piece ended up being stuck in his arm. He growled like an injured beast. I slipped my body from underneath him. He tried to get back on top of me. I managed to keep him away with a series of kicks, but not for long. He grabbed my ankles and squeezed them like they were marshmallows.

"Dead or alive!!!! It doesn't matter!" he snarled.

Frustrated, he removed the sharp object from his injured arm, then stabbed me multiple times with the sharp object. Then he planted it inside my ribs before grabbing me by the neck and starting to choke me again. His hands felt like iron claws, squeezing the life out of me. In a matter of seconds, I was lifeless in his hands, waiting for the end. Before I could pass out, he let me go. I was struggling to breathe. I slowly filled my lungs with air. That's when I felt his tongue swipe my clit. My body barely jerked in response to his touch as he began to eat me out like I was his last supper. Then he went on with a savage fisting like he was trying to remove a stain from the floor. I thought I couldn't feel any more pain at this point, but I was so wrong. The pain was immeasurable. He went back and forth like a locomotive on my lifeless body. With my legs spread wide, he took out his penis. He gave me a slap across my breasts. In a victorious tone, he said, "You're all mine."

He went on to savagely penetrate me, forcing his weight in with each stroke. He kept shouting obscenities while ravaging my vagina with the utmost aggressiveness. I kept my eyes on him.

My POV

They were filled with hate, judgment, and disgust for the vile creature that was on top of me. He didn't enjoy that. He shouted as he slapped me.

He took my dignity, my body, and my innocence.

"Look away, you trash!" he commanded.

I wouldn't give him this satisfaction. I turned my unwanted glare back at him with more combativeness. He didn't appreciate that one bit; he stopped. He got on top of me, lifted my hips, and screamed at me with spite, "Trying to be a tough one?"

He turned me around, lifted my hips up, and ripped the rest of my panties to brutally pound me in the asshole. I thought I couldn't feel any more pain with the way he rearranged every inch of me, but I was wrong. I could feel excrement coming in and out of my butt, yet it didn't stop him. He kept ramming me with my face halfway in the mud. In a vegetative state, he kept lifting me up by the hips without skipping a beat, destroying my butthole with full vigor. He went back inside my pussy. I could not determine the duration of that ordeal; time and space became irrelevant, and my knowledge or desire for knowledge ceased to hold significance. He went full throttle inside me, then I felt his semen fill my insides. I was lying lifeless with his cock still inside me. He removed it and went to give me a kiss on the cheek, then he whispered into my ear as the sound of thunder grumbled, "Death's better anyway; great ride, toots."

I passed out as he left me for dead on the ground. It didn't matter how far we as a human race went; we would always be a primitive species. We cast our own misery upon each other. How could we say we were smarter than animals? We had evolved, but somehow still acted in ways that blew my mind. Did we have a precondition to destroy each other? We knew millions of ways to kill each other, and we applied them with ease, willingly knowing that we also had the knowledge to do better. What was the point of being able to live in the present, know the past, and see the future if we kept acting like animals?

Chapter 10

My head ached, and I wondered why I was still conscious. I opened my eyes; my vision was blurry, allowing me to see only a few meters ahead. The weather had gotten worse; it was so cold that I could barely move. Struggling to breathe, I managed to crawl near a barricade to help myself stand up. I was near the bridge.

I took a thick branch to use as a cane. The beads of water kept falling one after another, without a sign of stopping. The rain had lost the ambient temperature of early fall, freezing and paling my skin on contact. It wasn't a pleasant coldness; it was the kind that made you walk all the faster and brace your head against the wind. I was drained. I was mentally and physically butchered, but I kept walking toward the bridge.

The growling sound of thunder, the wind shaking the trees, and the downpour was beating on the river with such aggression that it disturbed the flow of the water. Most of the bridge was submerged in water. The rapid water came colliding brutally with the old bridge; the roar coming from the waterfall was loud. During the severe weather, I continued to move forward despite being exhausted. Halfway across the bridge, it was getting harder to advance. Then I lost my balance and slipped. The current of the water was strong enough to pin my body against the wooden fence. On my butt, I sat there. I couldn't move anymore. Why bother? Why seek survival after such an awful, horrific, wicked experience that obliterated me to the core? Even if I wanted to, I couldn't externalize my pain. The sound of the brushing leaves whipping in the air, the wind blowing off everything in its passage, the water tearing apart the old bridge, and the rumbling of thunder screaming with such conviction made me feel small.

I looked at my bruised body. My life, my dreams, and all my unanswered questions were reaching their culmination. Unable to move my naked body, I wondered when death would claim me.

My POV

Would I meet a robed skeleton holding a scythe? Maybe I would go to Heaven or Hell. I could even be reincarnated, hopefully as someone or something awesome, or maybe I'd be stuck on this heartless rock as a ghost. I might even sleep for eternity.

The water moved my body; I could hear the wooden structure crack while my body followed the flow of the water. After a little travel, I stopped being carried. I lifted my head. I couldn't believe it. I was inches away from the bridge. I wasn't sure if it was by instinct, but I used my chin, trying to drag myself to safety.

Then, a ferociously loud lightning struck a tree near me; the tree snapped like a twig. Before I knew it, I had been propelled off the bridge. I submerged under the turbulent water; in there, I was engulfed in a cold quietness. I could hear the rhythm of my heart gradually fading. As I hit the bottom, I went into nothingness.

At least, that was what I thought.